PROM
TASTIC

To Giles

Scholastic Children's Books
A division of Scholastic Ltd
Euston House, 24 Eversholt Street
London, NW1 1DB, UK
Registered office: Westfield Road, Southam, Warwickshire, CV47 0RA
SCHOLASTIC and associated logos are trademarks and/or registered
trademarks of Scholastic Inc.

First published in the UK by Scholastic Ltd, 2015

Text copyright © Scholastic Ltd, 2015

ISBN 978 1407 15799 3

Printed by CPI Group (UK) Ltd, Croydon, CR0 4YY
Papers used by Scholastic Children's Books are made
from wood grown in sustainable forests.

3 5 7 9 10 8 6 4 2

www.scholastic.co.uk

LIZ ELWES

PROM TASTIC

■SCHOLASTIC

PART ONE

Prom Night – 7.50 p.m.

CHAPTER 1

Alex

7.50 p.m.

"Do you want to dance after the announcements?"

It was exactly like a film. And she was the lead actress for once, rather than the best friend.

He had asked her to dance.

As in come up to her *in front of everyone* and asked her to save him a dance. Had her "Yeah, sure" been calm enough? She was fretting it had been a bit squeaky but he had said "Cool" back, and smiled at her, so that was all right.

It was as if her fairy godmother had worked overtime to make this prom night the most magical evening of her life. Do wishing wands wear out? Hers must surely be about to. And the evening wasn't even finished yet. Her biggest wish, that special moment she had begun to think would never happen – that was still to come.

For once, she actually felt she looked pretty. Her wavy, dark brown hair was rippling smoothly down her back, thanks to Grace's rescue that afternoon. Her floating pale pink dress made her feel like a princess. Her silver heels were made for dancing, and shining on each of her nails were crystals identical to those decorating her dress. She really did feel like Cinderella at the ball.

And now the prince she had dreamed about for so long had asked her to dance. Her! Alex Robertson. She felt she was floating on air. She had seen the envious looks of some of the girls when he came up to her. She didn't blame them. Tonight she wouldn't have wanted to be anyone else. Not even Grace who was standing next to her, waiting to hear her name called out.

Everything leading up to this moment had been perfect. Being picked up from Grace's in the long white limo, coming out on to the red carpet. The huge Hollywood sign, the photographers taking photos of them with their fun fake Oscars, kneeling down to press their handprints in clay to make their prints. It had all been exactly like a Hollywood premiere and they were the stars.

She was standing in the middle of a room decorated top to bottom with massive photos of the Los Angeles skyline; above her golden stars spun amid clouds of pink and white balloons.

She knew that, at last, this was going to be her night.

Her Hollywood night.

She was going to have her first kiss.

And it was going to be just like in the films.

CHAPTER 2

Leigh

7.50 p.m.

It was obvious that she had either:

- died in an accident and was one hundred per cent *in hell*, or ...
- fallen into a massive coma and this was all a horrendous nightmare.

Leigh took a deep breath and squeezed her eyes tightly shut. "I am going to wake up any minute."

She slowly opened her eyes and looked down at her ripped dress, splattered with mud from top to bottom. Under her breath she cursed the stupid bus driver. She swore he had driven through that massive puddle on purpose. She glanced at her reflection in the large plate-glass window of a shop. An ambulance drove past, its flashing lights backlighting her toppled blonde hair, half an hour earlier so beautifully styled on the top of her head, now, falling off to one side like a blonde Marge Simpson in a strong wind.

The stormy light of the rain-swept street made her face look ghostly pale.

"Hey darlin', it's not Halloween tonight, is it?" A cackle of laughter followed a group of young men lolling out of a passing car. Leigh gave a wail of anguish, pain and frustration. She wanted to shout after them. "No, it's not Halloween, you jerks – it's my PROM NIGHT!"

She tried to make a rude gesture after the car but a spasm of pain shot up her arm and she flopped down hard on the wet pavement. She sat like a rag doll on the cold stone with both legs out in front of her. Her phone fell out of her bag, her tiny sparkly pale blush bag, now drenched in rain and speckled with dirt. She picked up her phone and hurled it into the bushes. Stupid, useless, broken phone. How could she be *here*? Outside in the rain when she should be *there*? How was anyone going to manage without her? It didn't seem possible that she wasn't at prom. This couldn't be happening. Not after all her hard work. Surely someone would miss her?

But she had a miserable feeling they wouldn't. She was alone. They would all be there. Without her.

The most important night of her life.

She sobbed into the cold, uncaring rain.

CHAPTER 3

Charlotte

7.50 p.m.

"Where is he?" She wondered as she scanned the room again.

He wasn't near the dance floor or the stage and she'd looked everywhere twice: under the green-and-pink neon Hollywood Cocktail Bar sign, by the striped candyfloss booth, at the hot-dog stand and next to the chocolate marshmallow fountain. She still didn't know what it was it all doing *here*. She was reeling with the effort of trying to process what was going on.

Why was she surrounded by everyone in her year dressed up in sequins and every colour of the rainbow? Why was her head teacher, Mrs Keane, up on stage banging a microphone trying to get it to work? None of this was supposed to be happening – not here, not at the Triangle.

What if the reason she was here was a scam, a sick joke? To her horror, she felt as if she might cry and she blundered against the crowd to find a chair in a darker part of the room to calm herself down. She pulled her shades down over her glossy dark fringe to cover her eyes, glad to hide her feelings behind them. As she so often did. She didn't care if shades were out of place here. She wasn't dressed for this. She was dressed for a quite different kind of evening. An evening with someone who hadn't shown up. Someone who had apparently thought it would be funny to send her here.

She slumped down on the chair and stuck her long, tanned legs in front of her, staring down at her black suede slouchy boots. She certainly stood out from the crowd dressed in a black minidress and grey silk vintage jacket. Even in her state of high agitation, the puzzled glances of her schoolmates had not gone unnoticed.

They must think she was crazy.

Unless they were all in on it and all laughing at her. She flashed a quick glance around the room, but from behind her shades she could see that everyone was occupied, staring up at Mrs Keane waving a gold envelope.

No one was looking at her.

She slowly got up from the chair. She wasn't going to be able to hold back those stupid tears any longer.

CHAPTER 4

Grace

7.50 p.m.

"Breathe. Just breathe."

Grace tried to take a deep breath but failed. She was too full of anxiety.

"Any minute now, Grace!" a voice yelled in her direction. Her heart pounded as the spotlight above her suddenly shot out a lightsabre beam, filling the distant stage with white glare.

At this signal, everyone around her rose like huge flock of birds: a flurry of multicoloured dresses and black tuxedos flying past, all heading in the same direction.

"Come on, Grace, you can't stay back here – you've got to be *close* when they announce it." Alex had grabbed her arm and was pulling her towards the lights.

"Shouldn't you find Evan?" Alex added.

Grace's heart took another lurch. The words wound her up as tightly as the strings on her violin. She *must* breathe: she could do it. *Just keep it steady, in and out,* she told herself.

"I don't know why you're looking nervous." Alex was now pushing her gently forwards. "You know it will be you. You're the most popular girl in the year. And ridiculously pretty. Now move before I have to kill you!"

I'm going to abandon breathing, Grace said to herself, *and concentrate on putting one foot in front of the other.* She was relieved when this seemed to work and she joined the drifting crowd.

"I voted for you!" a girl in her French class called over.

"Me too!" yelled Tom, as he gave her the thumbs

up. "And for Evan, of course – the swim team has to stick together."

She managed a fragile smile but she hardly heard a word.

Her whole life had been leading up to this moment. "It's going to be the best moment of your life," her mother had told her firmly. "It's your destiny."

And now here she was, in her stunning lace dress, her pale blonde hair beautifully styled. . .

"Grace! Bet you can't wait. You must be *so* excited. I voted for you both." Zoe pointed at two gold crowns sitting on a red velvet table, centre stage. Standing next to them was their head, Mrs Keane, banging the microphone trying to get it to work properly.

So it had arrived. The moment that had been entwined into her life story for about as long as she could remember.

"Grace!" Evan was standing in front of her. He grabbed her hand. He looked so tall and distinguished in his sharp black tuxedo, his blond hair smoothly styled back. His blue eyes stared straight down into hers.

The perfect Prom King. The perfect boyfriend.

She wound her fingers tightly round his.

She didn't know why she jumped like a startled cat when his name was announced and the room erupted into cheers. Of course it was Evan taking centre stage. Who else would it be?

Mrs Keane opened the second envelope.

"And the Prom Queen is. . ."

Mrs Keane paused for ever.

Grace felt her eyes boring into Mrs Keane's face.

"Say it! *Say it!*" she willed with all her might.

She said it.

Time stopped.

Alex's shocked face turned to her in slow motion.

"*What?*" she mouthed in disbelief.

Grace closed her eyes and took that deep breath at last.

CHAPTER 5

Kristyn

7.50 p.m.

Kristyn noticed Mrs Keane climbing up the stairs to the stage before anyone else did, before the spotlight was even turned on. She followed Mrs Keane's progress across the stage with her eyes. The lively buzz of the room seemed muted to Kristyn, as if she was wearing earmuffs. She found that she was holding her breath. When Mrs Keane pulled out the card for Prom Queen and read the name on it, a rush of noise washed over Kristyn, as if her imaginary earmuffs had suddenly been removed. She exhaled in a rush.

"It's me. It's really me," she whispered to herself.

Her name had been the one on the gold card.

In her fantasies she had climbed on to the stage and the boy standing next to her had moved towards her: he had looked at her with adoration, knowing she was the girl for him. And no one else in the room had stood a chance.

That was in her fantasies.

This was supposed to be moment that was going to make the whole of her life come right. The moment when she completely reinvented herself.

Surely she wasn't the only girl who had wished she could change herself. Who *hasn't* wished they hadn't said this or done that? Who *hasn't* sometimes wished they could wipe the slate clean and start again?

She glanced up at the golden stars hanging from the ceiling. The light danced off their glittery points. In the middle of each one was a photograph. She knew there was a shining star for every person at prom. Her own would be up there somewhere: twirling above her head. She remembered giving in her carefully chosen photo to Leigh. It seemed like a hundred years ago. If she had been told then she would be Prom Queen then, she would have laughed out loud.

Yet here she was, all her dreams come true. The Prom Queen. Evan at her side.

She scanned the crowd of faces staring up at her. Was it so terribly wrong not to want to be you? To be not the new girl who tried too hard to make friends, but the cool girl: the china-doll girl who never puts a foot wrong?

But she already knew the answer to that question.

Her heart was thumping as Mrs Keane picked up a crown. She looked out into the crowd: what would they say if they knew the kind of person she *really* was? What had made her do it? What had she been thinking? She pulled her gaze away from the hundreds of eyes on her and stared straight into the dazzling spotlight. Blinded by the beam, she imagined her star falling slowly from the ceiling and landing softly on the ground . . . then everyone deliberately drifting towards it and one by one crushing it under their heels.

PART TWO

29 Hours and 50 Minutes Earlier
– The Day Before Prom

CHAPTER 6

Leigh

2.00 p.m.

"Don't try and tell *me* I can't tell one pink from another. I know what colour I want those marshmallows and if you knew who you were dealing with you wouldn't even *say* the word 'raspberry' in the same breath as 'powder' to me."

Leigh opened her locker with her free hand and battled to pull a book out from the middle of a towering pile. Her other hand clamped her phone firmly to her ear. Failing to extract the book she needed, she tucked her phone between her chin and shoulder in order to wrest the French textbook free from the pile, then kicked the door shut with her foot. She slung the book into her bag, put the phone back to her ear and began to walk towards her lesson, ponytail swinging.

Charlotte came up alongside her, trying to attract her attention.

"No!" Leigh continued into the phone. "Raspberry pink is *not* the same as powder pink. Raspberry pink is practically a whole *universe* away from—"

Charlotte took her sleeve and mimed something at her.

Leigh pointed at the phone with her free hand, mouthing, "Not now."

Her friend raised her eyebrows and sighed.

Leigh saw Charlotte's face and felt bad but there was nothing she could do. She had left the marshmallows to someone else on the Prom Committee and look what had happened. If she wanted it done right, she would have to do it herself. All those months ago, when Leigh had volunteered to be on the committee, she hadn't seen it as work like some of the other girls, she had seen it as a golden opportunity. An opportunity not only to create the best prom the school had ever seen and show off her organizational skills, but also to have something to put on her CV to help get her into business school like her stepsister. She honestly couldn't remember a time when she wasn't making lists, sorting things out and working on timetables for homework or music lessons. She even liked to organize her free time into sections, though she would never admit that to anyone except Charlotte. Charlotte had laughed at her when she had found one of the timetables pinned up on the board in Leigh's bedroom. "Leigh, I cannot believe my eyes. Are you seriously telling me you timetable magazine-reading and exercise?"

"Yes," Leigh had replied firmly. "The word is *discipline*, Charlotte. I do two sessions of a high-intensity military-inspired training circuit every day. I need to keep fit."

"For Owen?"

"No, *not* for Owen. If I'm going to run my own business in the future I've got to get into good habits now. Exercise is important for keeping your mind quick." Leigh had paused and smiled. "OK, and I'm sure Owen appreciates it too."

"You've always had good habits, Leigh. Even in primary school you made Mrs Bishop give you the complete class timetable *and* gave her a hard time if she didn't stick to it."

"Well she was always trying to duck out of doing PE if it was only a tiny bit rainy!" Leigh had laughed.

Charlotte had grinned, "Please don't forget me when you're running the Bank of England or, even more useful to me, the TopShop empire."

"I won't – and don't forget *me* when you're a famous singer-songwriter."

"Would you be my manager?"

"Nah, I'm not into bands – too risky."

Leigh had ducked as Charlotte threw a pillow at her.

Owen was waiting for her outside French. He opened his mouth to speak and Leigh sighed as her phone began vibrating in her pocket again. She held out the palm of her hand to him, pulled a "Sorry" face and headed to take the call in the toilets along the corridor. If she got caught on the phone again at school she knew she'd be in trouble.

"Hello? Caterers? Right. I need to finalize the canapé selection. No, *no*! *Not* cocktail sausages."

If only everyone understood that she was doing it all for them, it would be such a help. Of course she couldn't be available to friends at the moment. But she was doing it to make the perfect evening for *them*. Why couldn't they see how important that was?

She ducked into French class just as the bell rang and shot Owen an apologetic smile as she slipped into her seat. She slid out one of her lists and slipped it into her French book. She began to highlight the things that were still left to do. The theme of the prom was Hollywood Nights and they already had the tea lights, fairy lights and the pretty white lacy metal centrepiece-holders all set up, but the stars still needed to be hung. Leigh highlighted "Hang stars" carefully in pink. Leigh had already bought the large jars for the sweets, the pink and white balloons, the stars, and the wallpaper of the LA skyline, but she drew a little arrow, pointing to the entry on her list that read "Hang LA skyline". Who was supposed to do that? She would have to check. The white flowers for centrepiece and decorations were ready as she had talked to the florist just that morning, so Leigh ticked that off. The steaks, burgers, fries, chilli dogs, Mississippi mud pie, doughnuts and frosted cupcakes were all ordered, though Leigh wanted to confirm the list with them one more time, as she wasn't fully convinced they had the order right. She highlighted that entry too. The dessert stations, ice cream and candyfloss stands, chocolate fountain and marshmallows were all officially confirmed though – at least there was that. She had to call the drinks people to make sure the Hollywood cocktail bar was on track, so she highlighted that as well. Leigh sighed. It still felt as if there was so much to do.

Each item on the list had its own sub-list of course with additional information, but that was on her laptop at home so she couldn't look at it now. Anyway, she knew it all by heart. It just made her feel good to see all the ticks next to the things that she had done and to think about how to sort out everything that was left. It was going to be perfect if she could just finish it all. She was proud of the way she had handled that crisis with the caterers. As if they had wanted cocktail sausages! That wasn't American-themed at all. She just wished that

Owen and Charlotte weren't so fed up with her for not being available.

"Leigh Kowalski!" She roused herself and sat up. Madame Blanc was standing over her. Before Leigh could clamp her hand over her list, Madame had snatched it up in her bony fingers. "*Voilà!* I see we are into *lists*, Leigh. Perhaps you would be so kind as to *list* ze vocabulary we 'ave been practising for ze past ten minutes."

Leigh wanted to say that unless that vocabulary included glitter, tablecloths or centrepieces she didn't really have a lot to offer in that department. "I'm sorry," she said instead. Wisely, she thought.

"I'm sorry too, Leigh." Madame folded the list and took it back to her desk. "Your concentration 'as been non-existent recently. Why can't you follow ze example of Zoe 'ere, who is always, *always*, paying attention?"

Zoe Anderson blushed scarlet, hung her head and looked as if she wanted to die.

Leigh knew that Zoe, as the shyest girl in the class, would have hated being singled out. "But, Madame!" Leigh protested.

Madame raised her hand. "I know, I know – prom, prom, prom. And I 'ave been very generous to you because I know this. But this is enough! Detention after school. Today."

"Today! But Madame, prom is tomorrow and I have so much still to do."

"Prom is one night; school is your whole future."

"Which shows how much *she* knows," Leigh moaned after class, walking towards the detention room with Owen. "I mean the night before prom and she *knows* there are last-minute changes that have had to be organized. It is *one* night, that's why it's *so* important – you only get one shot at making it perfect."

Owen stopped with her outside the detention-room door. "I could wait for you. Maybe after detention we could go for a coffee somewhere; it seems like I've hardly seen you—"

Leigh turned to him, incredulous. "Are you *mad*!? *Coffee!* I've just lost a whole hour off my schedule. I'll get to bed God knows when trying to make that time up. A nightmare! I'm never going to get through my list."

"Can I ask you something?" Owen sighed. "How can I get—"

The insistent buzz of Leigh's phone interrupted him. She held up a hand, indicating for him to wait. "Hello.

Right, yes, the marshmallows – oh, you can, brilliant. Of course the raspberry pink was completely wrong. Mmmm. . . Mmmm." She mouthed, "How can you get what?" at Owen, before barking, "Yes! Sun-dried tomatoes and olives," down her phone.

"Forget it." Owen turned and headed for the exit.

"Owen!" she called, watching his back as he disappeared down the corridor. She sighed to herself. They could have all the time they wanted together after tomorrow night.

She finished her call.

A text pinged up. It was from Owen.

How can I get on your list?

She looked at the number of missed calls from the caterers and the venue manager. She just didn't have enough time.

Her finger pressed "Ignore" on the text. Owen would have to wait.

CHAPTER 7

Grace

4.30 p.m.

"What do you think, Mum?" A tall girl appeared through the velvet changing-room curtains in a slinky silver dress and made a slow circle in front of the woman standing outside.

Sitting on the red silk sofa nearby, Grace's mum whispered to her daughter, "Marvellous . . . if you want to look like a giant Christmas cracker."

Grace frowned. "Mum! That girl's in my year. Be quiet!"

"Really?" Her mother examined her Chanel red nails, "I thought Maison Marie would be too expensive for most of your class. It *is* the best dress shop in town, after all." She looked again at the girl, who had raised her dress a little to show off some silver sandals. "Oh dear. Oh dear." Her mother leaned back on the deep cushions and flexed her own delicate ankles. "Let's face it, there aren't many girls who can carry off silver jersey. I mean, *you* could do it, of course, but then you've got the figure to wear anything. *Not*, I'm afraid" – her mum's voice dropped – "like Miss Lumpy over there . . . honestly, a couple of tubes of Pringles have to have better shape than those legs. . ."

"Mum! Will you *please* be quiet." Grace's embarrassment was saved by a saleswoman bustling towards them, a delicate gold-and-cream lace dress in its transparent plastic cover draped over one arm.

"We've done the alterations now and I think it's going to be simply perfect." The saleswoman beamed.

"Well, I should hope so – it was one of the most expensive in the shop."

Grace cringed again. All she could think about was how soon this fuss would be over. None of her friends at school had taken Friday afternoon off to get ready for prom but her mum had been insistent at breakfast. "There's so much to do, Grace. You simply won't have time on Saturday to do it all. And you've got to look the best."

"But what about my schoolwork?" Grace had asked, astonished. Usually this was a winning card: her mum was so determined that she was going to go to Oxford that there was never a let-up in her work schedule. This week alone she had her extra music, sports, and maths and English tuition.

"You've got to have a special something to stand out from the crowd. The competition for Oxford is ferocious," her mum had reminded her for the hundredth time.

"She does work hard," her dad said gently.

Her mum had whipped round on him. "She has to if she's going to make something of herself!"

"I'm just saying, Denise," her father had gone on patiently, "that sometimes I think she needs some time that isn't organized. . ."

"Don't be ridiculous, Doug! You have to push yourself in this life – perhaps that might have been a lesson for *your* career. Grace needs to understand that."

"But there's something extra every night," Grace had wailed, "and nearly all day Saturday when I have to get up early for sports club then extra maths, then violin practice. I can't remember ever having a lie-in, or a moment to myself. Every single day is planned out, every minute of my life . . . no time for . . . for me."

"I give you *some* time to see Evan, don't I? He's such a useful connection. It will all be worth it," her mum had said firmly. "We've got to make these sacrifices."

We! Grace had thought to herself.

Grace had given up on changing her mother's attitude. Because she was an only child, the spotlight of attention never wavered from her and there was nothing about her life that felt private.

Except one thing. She smiled quietly to herself – then gave herself a shake as she spotted the saleswoman looking enquiringly at her. She couldn't think about that now.

"Go on, then," her mother urged, pointing at the dress. "Try it on."

Now it was Grace's turn to emerge from behind the gold velvet curtains. Everyone in the shop stopped to stare.

Her mother's hands flew to her chest. "Grace, you look beautiful." She stood up as if to put her arms round her, but thought better of disturbing her hair and dress and patted her on the arm instead. "There won't be a another girl in the school to touch you."

A few other mums and daughters in the shop eyed one another at this, but that afternoon in Maison Marie no one could deny that Grace looked stunning.

The cream silk covered in filigree gold and cream lace swished gently as she turned in front of the mirror.

"French lace really is the best, Mrs Gardener. Worth the expense," the saleswoman gushed admiringly.

"Nothing but the best for my daughter." Grace's mum took out a tissue. "She's nearly all grown-up now."

Yes, I am, Grace thought to herself back in the changing room as she let the dress slip off her shoulders. *So why do you still treat me like a child?*

But she meekly handed the dress over to be wrapped

and pulled on her jeans and white T-shirt. As she picked up her pink cardigan, her phone rang.

"Hi! *HELLO!* magazine here, calling Grace Gardener for an interview."

"Hi, Alex, where are you?"

"You mean, where are *you*? Lucky thing, getting the afternoon off. While I've suffered the most *très* boring French lesson *dans le monde*, you've been swanning around being beautified. Are you at this minute lying on a sofa being fed chocs and champagne at Maison Marie?"

"We're very nearly done here."

"Is the dress dreamy amazingness?"

"It *is* lovely."

"So what else have you been doing? Please, please tell me everything went wrong at the tanning shop and you look like an Oompa-Loompa."

"Shut up!"

"Come on. Spill. I'm just about to put my feet into Mum's massaging foot spa with a ton of softening oil, so I'm immobile for at least ten minutes."

"OK, OK. Well, the tan is done and I'm only slightly carrot-coloured. I've had a manicure. That was pretty nice, actually. I went for pale gold with a slightly sparkly topcoat. Then I spent a lifetime in the Style House while they covered me in foils and made me look like an alien."

"Did you get a head massage when you got it washed?"

"Yes – that *was* great. And I had freshly squeezed apple-and-mango juice and a smoked-salmon panini."

"Noooo! At Tillie's Tresses you're lucky if you get a PG Tips and a stale digestive."

Grace laughed. "Now you know you're having your hair done at the Style House tomorrow, so don't pretend you aren't going to look amazing. Every salon in town is booked solid. I can't wait to see everyone."

There was a moment's pause before Alex said quietly, "This is really it, isn't it, Grace? This is what we've been looking forward to since our first day at secondary school. Now we're leaving Harper High and going to be all grown-up."

"I know. It's like the first day of the rest of our lives."

"At least you've managed to get a boyfriend before you leave school."

"You will too."

There was another pause.

"Are we still meeting at the cinema tonight?"

"Of course. Evan's coming too."

"You are lucky your mum loves him so much."

"She loves the fact his dad's a top lawyer," Grace said curtly.

"And that he's trying for Oxford, like you," Alex added.

"That too."

"And that he's incredibly good-looking, hard-working, on the swim team and – Hello? I think that's what's called a perfect boy."

"My mother is *too* keen on our relationship and when he turns up she's going to go on and on to everyone in the shop about what a marvellous couple we make."

"But you *dooo*."

"It's embarrassing."

"Grace! Grace!" her mother was shouting outside. "Are you decent?" Grace heard her mother give a girlish giggle. "Evan is here."

CHAPTER 8

Kristyn

4.45 p.m.

Kristyn hadn't intended to follow Evan from school to Maison Marie: that would have made her some kind of crazy stalker. But when he had turned into the shop, she couldn't help going in too. After all, she did still need shoes for prom. Maybe she could check out the designer shoes and try to customize a cheaper pair. Or maybe she could even afford some nicer ones, if she borrowed some money from her parents. She was starting a new well-paid waitressing job tonight and she'd be able to pay them back quickly. She had worked so hard for the past four months at the coffee bar to repay them for her prom dress; maybe they'd be willing to lend her some money for shoes now. The thought of her dress hanging on her wardrobe door made her feel happy. She had got it online. A one-off vintage find. She knew no one else would have one like it. She did have a knack for spotting amazing finds like this dress. Her dream was to be a stylist but she had no idea how she could make it happen. "Why bother going to college to study some more?" her older sister always said. "I'll get you a job in the salon and you can earn some decent money." And her parents always agreed with Jessie.

The shop doorbell jangled loudly as she went in, making her jump – but Evan was already disappearing into the back where all the dresses and tuxedos were and luckily he didn't turn round.

Each pair of shoes was carefully displayed like Cinderella's glass slippers. She picked up the nearest shoe, and turned over a handwritten price tag tied to the ankle strap with thin gold ribbon. Her eyes widened: £560.00! She hastily placed it back on its gold velvet cushion. She was sure the sales assistant with the scary painted black eyebrows had seen her reaction and was now sneering at her. She watched her go over to the girl at the till and say something. The girl smirked. Kristyn wanted to run out of the shop, but instead she picked up another shoe – slightly less expensive but still way, way out of her price range.

She wondered, not for the first time, why posh shops were always so *quiet*. Was it the rich velvet curtains, or the thick carpet she could feel her cheap school shoes sinking into? In the silence she felt the stares of the staff burning into the back of her neck like lasers as she pretended to consider a pair of delicate Jimmy Choo heels.

"Would you like to try those on?" It was Scary Eyebrows, who had drifted noiselessly to her side.

Before she knew it she had said firmly, "Yes, please."

What was she doing?! Now she had made things worse, because both she and the sales assistant knew this was going nowhere. But she had started the game and Evan was in the shop and might come back at any minute. If he saw her he might stop to say hello. Possibly. She wondered why he had come in here. Picking up his tuxedo?

"Do sit down," the sales assistant sighed, gesturing to one of the beautiful gold chairs, upholstered in red silk, "and I'll get them for you. What size?"

Kristyn told her and took a seat, her back to the archway that led to the dress section. If she looked in the gilt-edged mirror in front of her she would see the reflection of anyone coming or going. If Evan came out she could casually get up and say something.

As she began to practise what she actually *would* say, a loud voice in the dress department pierced the quiet. "Grace, you looked an absolute *angel* in that dress. I know I keep saying it – but she did. You just wait, Evan!"

Grace. It would be. Kristyn felt disappointed with herself for not guessing sooner. Of course that would be why Evan was here.

"Mum, are we finished now? I'm exhausted after everything this afternoon and we're going to see that film later." She heard Grace's clear voice.

"Yes, we're done now, *finally*. See why you needed

to take the afternoon off school? There was just so much to be done. It's cost the earth, but you are worth it, and it's a once-in-a-lifetime night. Now, tomorrow we've got the hairdresser booked for final blow-dry with dress *on*. Maison Marie are sending the dress to the salon. Then the after-prom party at our house; I've ordered catering from Carousel. We've got the limo ordered, of course, but there's so much still to do. Why don't you and Evan go and have some something at Café Luigi's after the film?"

"Luigi's?" Grace sounded unimpressed. "Well, OK. That would be nice."

"You can make up the study time later, but I know you and Evan need some time alone . . . although, straight back after, please. You've still got a lot to do today to prepare for your tutorial tomorrow, and your music practice. And *definitely* don't order pasta, Grace. Promise me? And don't eat the bread. You want to fit into that dress tomorrow, don't you?"

In the mirror Kristyn saw Grace appear with Evan, followed by Grace's mother. Her hands gripping the side of the chair, Kristyn sank down into the seat and clenched her eyes shut. The doorbell clanged and they were gone.

When she opened her eyes again the sales assistant was staring down at her. She shuffled back up the chair with as much dignity as she could, silently praying that the assistant was going to tell her they didn't have the shoes in her size, so she could get out of the shop as fast as possible. They both knew she wasn't going to buy them. She wished her mum was there. She couldn't count the times she had asked her mum to go shopping with her. "Oh, Kristyn, I would – but I'm working."

Her mum was always working. Her new job at the care home meant long hours, and her dad's warehouse hours demanded long shifts as well. And of course Jessie had her job at the Style House. It was her dad's work that had caused them to move to this town. Nobody appeared to notice that arriving new at Harper High at the beginning of the year had been hard for her. Certainly her family were all much too busy to pay any attention to the fact that it was her prom tomorrow. She considered the conversation she'd just overheard and felt a pang of sadness. How great it must be to have a mother who took you out of school to treat and pamper you. No older sister to take all the attention, either. Grace didn't realize how lucky she was. No wiping tables for *her*. Everyone else seemed to have all the luck. While Kristyn, it seemed, could never catch a break. Really, was it too much to ask? Just *one break*.

The saleswoman held out a pair of black satin heels. "You're a very lucky girl," she said flatly. "They were the very last pair in your size."

"Of course they were," Kristyn sighed and began pulling off her school shoes.

CHAPTER 9

Charlotte

4.45 p.m.

"Yes, well, I'd like to be on your list too, Leigh."
Charlotte had finished her after-school guitar lesson
and was sitting on the wall with her by the bus stop.

"What? Oh don't *you* start, as well. It's bad enough
that detention set me back an hour. I didn't have time
for coffee."

"An hour, you say!" Charlotte crammed a black
beret on her head. "OMG! Call Superman – perhaps
he can spin the earth in reverse for you!"

Leigh looked at Charlotte, her blue eyes narrowed. "You really have no idea, do you."

"I know it seems to be a lot of fuss about nothing very important." Leigh choked on her crisps – but Charlotte wasn't finished. "I mean, what is prom? What is it really? Just a night where everyone gets together, has a bit to eat and drink and has a dance. Oh, and not forgetting the ridiculous popularity competition for Prom King and Queen. Like *that's* going to be a surprise . . . not."

Leigh brushed a bit of crisp off her shirt. "Well, that's all you know. For everyone else except *you*, Miss Party Pooper, it's a never-to-be-forgotten night, a magical night—"

"Oh please!"

"A *magical* night where dreams really can come true. A rite of passage. It marks the end of one part of your life and the beginning of another. And you're saying that's not worth making a fuss about?"

"I know it's important to you, Leigh, and I am trying to respect that."

Leigh raised her eyebrows, sniffed and popped another crisp into her mouth.

Charlotte went on, "But you need to respect that it's simply not important to *me*. What could be important about which vehicle you're arriving in: limo, bus, Ferrari, skateboard . . . what does it matter? Just a chance for people to make money out of you. Who cares where you got your dress and how much it cost and where you're getting your hair done and who your date might be? It's all so . . . so . . . *superficial*."

"Well, lots of people do care, actually – because they think it's important to mark change in their lives. It should be celebrated in a special way. It's fun thing to do, to feel special, like a film star. Most of us don't lead film-star lives and for one night we can dress up and feel glamorous and know it's our night. Honestly, Charlotte, you'll regret it if you don't come, you truly will. Please come. Pleeeeease? For me?"

Not this again. Charlotte was grateful to see her bus arrive. She gave Leigh a quick hug, flung her bag over her shoulder and hopped on. "I'm just not interested in all the prama." That was her word for all the craziness going on around prom. Thank goodness it was all going to be over tomorrow and then they could all get back to normal.

Charlotte got out her notebook and pencil. She wanted to get down some lyrics about what she was feeling at the moment. Angry, frustrated and, she suddenly realized, alone. She missed Leigh. The Leigh-before-prom. But she missed something else as well – and the weird thing was she wasn't even sure what it was. . .

She knew what Leigh would say. Leigh would say it was a boy. But that was crazy.

How can you miss a boy you've never met?

The bus pulled up in front of the coffee shop.

"You're so not going to believe my sick idea!"

She looked up from her notebook to see two girls from her year, Lexie and Lindsay, clambering into the empty seats at the front. They hadn't seen her because of the enormous man sitting in front of her and she was glad; those two were not her favourite people.

"I've got this brilliant plan!" Lindsay shrieked. "A *fake* promposal! It would be such a laugh, wouldn't it?"

"But who would you do it to? And what would you do?" Lexie sounded perplexed.

"I'm not sure yet. Someone who is lame enough not

to have already been invited. I'm going to have to think about it. Maybe one of those stuck-up girls who think they're so clever. And suck up to teachers all the time. Someone who Mrs McDonnell likes – because she's the one that's got me chucked out of prom."

"Unless you pass that history test."

"Yeah, we all know she thinks that's not going to happen unless a there's a miracle. She doesn't want me there. Stupid cow! My mum even went into school to say it was unfair, but – can you believe it? They wouldn't listen! Mrs Keane said my attendance had been so poor and my mark on that last history test was so bad. . ."

"You did have quite a lot of warnings before that. . ."

"Yeah, I *know*, but I didn't think they'd actually have the nerve to *do* it! Ban someone from their own prom?! That's got to be against my human rights or something."

"You could study really hard for the test tonight," Lexie ventured.

"It's at midday tomorrow! Mrs McDonnell is coming in specially. Jed's got to do it too. He's also on last warning for prom. Imagine Jed not being at prom."

"So you're going to revise tonight, then?" Lexie knew, although she would never dare say it, that Lindsay had a big crush on Jed and had high hopes they would get together at prom.

"Are you kidding! I've got a better plan than that. I've just spotted Kristyn in Maison Marie. Don't know why she was there – way out of *her* league."

Charlotte made a face. She sometimes wondered why Kristyn hung out with Lindsay; Kristyn seemed like a nice enough girl and she was so much smarter than Lindsay.

"So?" Lexie asked.

"And she aced that history test. I'm going round to pick it up from her house tonight. She thinks it's for revision but I'm going to sneak it in."

"You'll get caught."

"No I won't. I'm clever like that. Remember when I nicked that make-up from the chemist's?" Lindsay waggled her fingers, "I'm like a magician! I'll be at that prom, don't you worry. Now, about that fake promposal; we've only got tomorrow. Let's see . . . who do I know who it would be a laugh to make a fool out of?"

"Can't we talk about who we think is going to have the worst dress instead?" Lexie asked, feeling that was safer ground.

Charlotte pulled her beret down over her eyes and leaned against the bus window. She thought for the millionth time how completely right she was to hate prom and every single thing about it. If only she wasn't the only person in the whole school who felt that way.

CHAPTER 10

Kristyn

5.00 p.m.

Kristyn was staring at her feet in the Jimmy Choo shoes. The delicate heeled sandals were beautiful and there was no doubt that they would look perfect with her dress. She would have a look down the market tomorrow to see if she could find anything similar. Shoes were important, but her dress was so lovely that she wasn't going to stress too much about any other part of her outfit. Her long dark auburn hair and green eyes would stand out against the pure white satin. There were silver sequinned straps and a ribbon of sequins under the bustline. It was so stylish. For the first time she wouldn't feel "second best" to everyone at school. Even Jessie had admired it, had actually asked to *borrow* it when it arrived. Kristyn had said firmly, "Absolutely, one hundred per cent *no*. It's my special dress and *I'm* going to be the first to wear it."

The door of Maison Marie jangling behind her making her jump again.

"Kristyn! I thought I saw you in the window." Lindsay looked at her shoes. "Wow, cool. Are you going to get those?" She didn't try to hide the surprise in her voice.

Kristyn looked at Scary Eyebrows: time for their little game to finish. "No," she said firmly. "They aren't quite right."

The sales assistant smirked knowingly.

Kristyn blushed and bent down to take them off.

Lindsay flopped down in the chair next to her. "What are you doing here? Bit late for prom shopping."

"Just looking for shoe ideas. I have a pair I could wear, but I don't know if they're right with my dress."

"Saw Grace and Evan on a date just now. Her mum handing over the dosh. I suppose that's one way to keep a boyfriend."

"What do you mean?"

"Get your mum to pay for your dates. I think most boys wouldn't complain about that."

"I don't think Evan is actually like that," Kristyn said warily. She didn't want to offend Lindsay, who took every opportunity to point out that she was the only real friend Kristyn had at school. She finished unstrapping the Jimmy Choos and handed them to the sales assistant.

"Suppose not." Lindsay pulled a face. "But still, it must help. I can't see what he sees in her.'

Kristyn raised her eyebrows. Even *she,* who was mad about Evan, could see what he saw in Grace.

"OK, she's *quite* pretty. But hey, we could all look good if our mum spent as much money on us as hers does. I bet she's had the works done before this prom and with no expense spared."

"Mmm. . ." Kristyn murmured. "I heard them in

here just now – she's been everywhere today, top-to-toe pampering. . ."

Lindsay pounced on this information. "Of course she has. How can anyone else compete with Princess Perfect? Swanking around school showing off that she's going out with Evan."

"She doesn't *really*. . ."

"She's so full of herself. She's not even that bothered about prom. Lexie heard her telling someone she'll be glad when all the fuss is over. Can you believe it! Maybe she's just using him so she can be Prom Queen. It's like she doesn't even care about *him*, just the crown."

That dart struck home. "It's not fair if she doesn't appreciate him," Kristyn said hotly. "He's not just good-looking; he's always so nice to everyone, and funny. . . like when he talks to you – as if you're the only person in the world. . ." Kristyn stopped herself; she was giving away too much. Too late.

"You're so right. He should go out with someone like *you*. Someone who could really appreciate him, someone who doesn't take things for granted. Grace does, doesn't she? Everything just gets given to her; she doesn't have to work for anything. You wouldn't see her working in a coffee bar, cleaning tables. . ."

Kristyn blushed; she wished she hadn't told Lindsay about that. That time that Evan had come into the coffee bar with Chris, and she had been standing over a dirty bucket mopping the floor. In her brown nylon apron. She blushed at the memory. She had felt so humiliated. It's not exactly how you want the boy of your dreams to see you. Chris had started nudging and pointing at her, but Evan had shut him up and been so charming and friendly he had almost made her feel that cleaning the floor was the best job in the world. . . That was the kind of boy Evan was – but it stung to know he would never see *Grace* with a dishcloth in her hand, wiping coffee stains and cake crumbs off tables. *She* would probably be having a tray of breakfast tea and toast brought to her in bed on Saturday mornings, white linen pillows plumped behind her while she watched all her favourite programmes.

Kristyn thought of all the early weekend mornings she had wanted to stay in *her* warm bed and had had to get up, catch a bus, put on an apron and start washing up and cleaning tables. Grace simply swans into this swanky boutique and her mum buys her the most expensive dress in the shop. It just didn't seem fair!

"It's not fair!" Lindsay cried. Kristyn swung round, surprised to hear her thoughts spoken out loud. "It's not fair that a girl like Grace gets to go to prom with Evan, when you are so much more genuine than her. She's so spoiled – but you, you really value how important your friends are. You are a truly *loyal* person. I think you're an exact match for Evan – you're *so* kind to people and always try to help your friends out. You'd be *such* a good couple. Whereas Grace doesn't know what wanting something and having to work hard for it is like. Living her dreamy princess life and not appreciating a thing about it."

Kristyn thought about Grace's tone of voice as she left the shop. She had sounded tired. As if she was under some kind of strain! As if!

"It's also *so* not fair I've got to pass this stupid history test or miss prom. Can you imagine that? Me, miss prom? I'm going to have to work all night revising for it. In fact I'd better go now." Lindsay let out a great sigh and suddenly looked close to tears.

"Don't worry," Kristyn soothed, as she pulled her school shoes on. "If you really work you will pass that test."

Lindsay got out a tissue. "It's just that I've lost all my notes – I think my dog might have been at my things or something . . . I can't find them anywhere."

"Lost all your notes?" Kristyn gasped. "But how are you going to revise?"

"What I really need is that history paper – but one that someone did well on. So I can use their answers to revise from."

Kristyn paused. She didn't feel very comfortable giving out her paper – but Lindsay *was* her friend, wasn't she?

"Well . . . you can have mine, but I'm working later tonight, so you'd have to come now."

"Can't. I'm not free – something I've got to do – but I can come and get it from your house later."

"I suppose I can ask my mum to give it to you if I leave it by the door."

Lindsay jumped up. "Thanks, Kristyn – you're a star. I told you you were a great friend. Got to dash now . . . meeting Lexie." As she reached the shop door she turned round. "Will Jessie be in?"

Kristyn, who was putting on her jacket, tensed. "She might be, but I've told you, she won't do any of my friends' hair for free. I *did* ask her."

"OK, just *wondered*!" Lindsay opened the door, "Bye-ee!" she cried over the jangling bell as she disappeared into the street.

As Kristyn too escaped into the sunshine, her phone rang.

"Hello – Mum? What's up?"

"Kristyn? Where are you?"

"Mum! What's the matter? You sound weird. Are you OK?"

"Yes. Everyone's OK. No one's hurt or anything like that. It's just that something's happened."

"What? What's happened, Mum?"

"Before I tell you, you need to know that Jessie is very, very sorry."

CHAPTER 11

Alex

6.30 p.m.

Alex wondered if the kiss was ever going to happen.

Taylor Lautner always made her heart beat faster, and now it was the moment she had been waiting for. He was leaning in, his eyes fluttering shut . . . she was actually feeling a bit giddy. . .

"Popcorn?" Grace shoved a red-and-white-striped bucket in front of her.

Alex nearly jumped out of her red plush seat. "No, thanks."

It was all right for Grace. Grace was cosily sitting next to Evan. Alex was sitting next to no one and therefore had to study the world of romance by watching films like these.

The way things were at the moment, it was the closest she was going to get – and why? She had never even been asked out by a boy. At this thought Alex changed her mind, took a huge scoop of popcorn in one hand and began popping it mechanically into her mouth, piece by piece, with the other. She might as well not worry about eating healthy food. At this rate she was going to die alone, in a dingy flat, a grey old lady probably found eaten by her cats and on her tombstone they would write, "Here lies Alex Robertson WHO NEVER HAD A BOYFRIEND."

What was wrong with her? Alex stopped herself. She didn't want to go down *that* road or she'd be sitting in this cinema all night working out the list she already knew too well. And adding extra bits too.

"You worry too much." Alex's mum had told her that morning as she handed her some toast.

Not for the first time, Alex wished her mum didn't have a spooky way of knowing what was on her mind.

"You go to prom and you'll have a lovely time, you'll see. I wish I could make you believe what a pretty girl you are."

"Ooh. Steady, Mum. We mustn't give false hope. . ."

Alex hit her younger brother on the arm.

"Very funny, Harry. Ha. Ha. Thirteen is such a *hilarious* age, is it not?"

Harry waved his slice of hot buttered toast, dripping with strawberry jam, dangerously close to her face.

"Stop it, you two." Her mum sat down at the table. She pushed aside the butter and chocolate spread to make room for a white plate with a grilled steak in the middle of it.

"No carbs is it today, Mum?" Alex asked.

"That's right, it's protein, protein, protein for me all the way from now on."

"Just protein?" Harry frowned. "That doesn't sound too healthy."

"And oranges."

Alex and Harry grinned at each other. Their mum

had complained she had to lose a stone for as long as they could remember.

"What happened to the big bowl of porridge for breakfast yesterday? Er . . . the high-fibre diet, wasn't it?" Alex asked innocently.

"I'm not sure." Harry grinned. "I think I saw a Kit-Kat wrapper in the bin last night."

"Actually" – her mother pushed her dark curls off her kind face – "we're not talking about *me*, we're talking about *you*, and how you are going to have a such wonderful time at prom. You're a beautiful girl. Shut up, Harry." She took her Alex's face in her hands. "I want you to know this. I swear without a doubt one day soon a boy will ask you out. A boy you really, really like. There is no doubt about it. It's the way of the world. What a lot of time you girls waste worrying about if and when it's going to happen. *It's going to happen!* I solemnly swear on my sacred weighing scales. Trust me. I know. I'm very old and wise. So stop stressing and enjoy yourself in the meantime, you gorgeous girl!" Her mum gave her a huge hug.

Harry got up and edged behind Alex. "I'd keep worrying if I were you," he whispered as he nicked the last piece of toast from her plate.

"*Harry!*" her mum yelled.

However, sitting in the dark in the cinema with the world's most perfect couple on screen and the school's most perfect couple sitting next to you, it was hard to believe her mum. What did she know? Nearly everyone else at school had at been asked out at least once. She was finding it increasingly hard to force herself to join in all their chatter as if she hadn't a care in the world.

Even today in art they had been talking about dating and she had been acutely aware that Chris was in the room with them. The boy she had told no one she'd had a crush on for the last five years. Trouble was, she wasn't alone. Lots of girls liked him – and who could blame them? He was fit, athletic, with thick blond hair and blue eyes, and bursting with self-confidence.

They had been drawing a huge pottery jug overflowing with white chrysanthemums.

"What's everyone's favourite flower?" Alex's friend Tom had asked the art room in general.

"Red roses," Alex had blurted straight out without thinking. Then she'd blushed furiously because she knew Chris could hear. She had accidentally caught his eye and he'd winked at her.

"Red roses, huh? Good to know," he had said.

Of course she agonized for the rest of the art lesson in case "roses" was a stupid answer. They truly were her favourite flower but now she wished she'd said, "Tulips" or even "Orchids", like Charlotte. "Roses" now seemed dull and a bit ridiculous. Had Chris been laughing at her? She wished Tom had never asked the question.

Alex had noticed Lexie and Lindsay looking at her table, giggling and nudging each other. If only Chris hadn't heard her. Now he'd think she was just as boring as her flower choice. Oh why, oh why had she said "roses"?

She made an effort to forget all flower-related thoughts and concentrate instead on the film on the screen. She knew true romance existed in real life because otherwise why would they bother to make so many films about it? Not for the first time she was grateful that Grace and Evan weren't into any public displays of affection. They were always very considerate about that and she wondered if it was because Grace knew that she had never kissed a boy.

"Don't worry about it," Grace always said. "I promise you when it happens you'll know what to do."

All very well for you not to worry. Alex had thought to herself. *You have a boyfriend, you've kissed him a thousand times probably. Kissing is nothing to you – you KNOW HOW TO DO IT. But what if you don't? What if your teeth clash, what happens if your noses bump, what about getting the angle right?* Alex wasn't sure that anyone had mentioned angles before as a possible area of disaster, but it worried her that she might go the wrong way and end up kissing an ear. Grace had assured her that none of these things mattered, *if it was the right boy.* Well, at least she was sure about *that.*

"There is someone for everyone." Taylor Lautner said on the screen.

She hoped Taylor was right. And her mum. In the dark of the cinema she crossed her fingers and made a wish.

CHAPTER 12

Grace

8.00 p.m.

Grace was pleased Café Luigi was quiet. The waiter took them to a table covered in a plastic red-and-white tablecloth, on which a candle flickered. The dark orange walls were lined with wine bottles and badly painted pictures of Italy. Grace liked Luigi's: the waiters were friendly and didn't make her feel uncomfortable and small, the way the waiters did at the smart places where her mum liked to be seen.

"It was nice of your mum to offer to treat us," Evan said, looking at the menu.

"Well, she would. She thinks you're practically a god."

Evan frowned. "And that's a bad thing? I thought that was the whole point?"

"Yes, well of course it's a good thing. It *has been* a good thing, but. . ."

"But what?"

Grace sighed and put her napkin on her lap. "It's been a long day. How's it going with *your* parents?"

Evan pushed his hand through his blond hair and shrugged. "Same old, same old. . . Oxbridge blah blah. Work harder, work harder . . . take on more at school, swim team, debating. It's going to get worse at sixth-form college. It's as if all they care about is me going to Oxford. I honestly think if I don't get there they'll never feel the same about me again. Especially my dad – I'll be a failure in his eyes for ever after."

"I know. I really wanted to go at first, but lately I feel like I'm doing it for my mum, not for me at all."

"Me too. And it's worse not having brothers or

sisters. It's all on me. No room for anything other than perfection. That's why they love me going out with you. The perfect couple."

Grace looked at the menu. "Our parents think we are." She looked up at him again. "Evan, I worry that you push yourself so hard trying to be the faultless son. You don't have to be the best at everything."

"Yes I do. And I could say exactly the same to you. But I have to try harder even than you." He gave her a long stare. "And you know why."

"Oh, Evan," she sighed.

They were interrupted by the waiter arriving to take their order.

"One lasagne and one mushroom linguini please," Grace said firmly, "and two Cokes. And some bread, please."

"Certainly!" The waiter beamed at them and disappeared.

"Well, *he* thinks we're great together, doesn't he?" Evan smiled.

"*Everyone* thinks we're a great together, Evan," Grace said sharply. "Hasn't that been the whole point of the past six months?"

"I know, Grace. I know. But I can't see another way for me . . . not yet."

"Yes, you can! You can!" She leaned forward. "You have to. You can't go on like this and *I* can't go on like this. I just can't do it any more."

Evan went pale. "Grace. . ."

"No, listen to me. This whole prom night has got me thinking. We're growing up. We're not kids any more. We can't spend the rest of our lives being someone just because it pleases our parents. We have to stop this sometime. This prom means we're moving on. *I've* got to move on. And so have you."

"But Grace. Do you know what that means? It's easier for you. I've got so much more to lose. . ."

Grace grabbed his hands. "No! You've got so much more to *gain*. Don't you see? No more lying. . . Can't you imagine the relief? Just to be truly yourself."

"You mean be gay."

Grace paused. "I mean be *you*, Evan. And if being gay is a part of being you, the time has come to own it. Be proud of it."

Evan leaned back in his chair and gave a hollow laugh. "And do you think my dad will be proud of it? My mates on the swim team? Guys like Tom and Chris? Do you think they'll be *proud* of it?"

"Your parents will come round. They love you. They'll have to accept it. And as for people at school, the ones worth knowing will still be your friends. The rest won't deserve to be and you'll be well rid of them."

"That's so easy for you to say, Grace, but I really like all my mates. I *like* hanging around with them. They think I'm cool because I'm your boyfriend. What if they don't want to know me once they find out that's fake? That's too much to lose."

"They like you for *you*! Nothing to do with me. And if they don't accept all of you, then they're not worth it. Life is full of risks, and I understand that you see coming out as a huge risk. But it's not. The risk is spending the rest of your life terrified and hiding who you truly are, wondering if and when you're going to get found out. Now that *is* what I call a risk."

Evan put his face in his hands. "Oh God, even *thinking* about telling my dad, and my mum. . ."

Grace's voice softened. "I'm not saying it's not going to be tough, but I'm here for you. And it's not going to stop you going to Oxford, is it? Just imagine the relief of having nothing to hide any more. Imagine that."

He put his hands on the table. "You're right. You're right." His blue eyes looked into hers. "I owe you, Grace, for agreeing to this messed-up relationship in the first place. You're the most understanding person I know; I can't imagine any other girl would have done it. I can't even imagine having told anyone but you." Evan sighed.

"Evan, you're one of my best friends and I'm so glad you did tell me. But remember, I had my *own* reasons for agreeing to this relationship," Grace responded swiftly. "It wasn't all me being kind. It worked both ways – but as I said, prom night has made me rethink what we're doing. . ."

Evan nodded. "So when are you going to tell the world *your* secret? God, your mum will *not* be pleased."

"I don't know – but I know I've got to stand up for myself one day."

"But not before prom?" His put his hands together as if he was praying. "I know it's a big, big ask. . ."

Grace sighed, but Evan was her friend. And she was

loyal to her friends. Whatever the cost.

"Please? I'm *begging* you. I really am. Let's wait until after graduation. I just need a bit more time."

Grace saw the fear and desperation in his eyes and sighed. "OK."

"As soon as we leave school, I swear I'll come out and all this fake life will be finished."

"Promise, Evan?"

"Promise, Grace."

But she hardly heard him. She was already thinking about another conversation she was now going to have to have.

And she wasn't looking forward to it.

CHAPTER 13

Leigh

8.30 p.m.

Leigh hated the feeling that Owen was angry with her. Owen was *never* angry with her. Owen was always so chilled; he found her need to organize everything cute. He never got annoyed at her for wanting to do things properly.

She warmed to the memory of him laughing when she chased him around her room trying to straighten out that stubborn kink in his thick, dark hair, the one that stuck out over the back of his collar. "Gerroff, you nutter!" he had grinned, shielding himself with his school bag.

No. Owen couldn't really be angry with her.

He would get over it once prom was done. It was only for now. When he realized it had been the most perfect prom ever, he would understand why Leigh hadn't had time for anything else. She looked at the big mahogany dining table in front of her. Her laptop lay in the middle of it: the mother ship. Surrounding it, covering every inch of the large table, were spreadsheets, timetables, highlighters, menus, invitation lists and "To do" lists. She thought that getting everything out would make her feel calmer, but now she was looking at it all she felt a rising sense of panic. It *had* to be perfect. What was the point of organizing something if it wasn't the very, very best? If everyone didn't say the next day, "Wasn't that the best prom ever?"

What had she said to Owen this morning? She was stressing about the last-minute changes and had overheard him murmur quietly that it wasn't as if someone was getting married or anything. She flinched slightly as she remembered her withering tone as she had snapped, "No, Owen, it isn't. Because when you get *married* and it doesn't work out you can have another wedding. It may have escaped your notice but you can't do prom twice. You only get *one* shot at it. *That's* why it's important."

"More important than me?" he had snapped back. She hadn't given him an answer, and he had stormed off.

Thinking about that conversation made her feel uncomfortable. She needed to forget about it or she wouldn't be able to get on with all the things she still needed to do.

She picked up a note.

Red-and-white-striped awning material
for candyfloss and hot dog booths

Georgia's dad worked at the market and was bringing that to school tomorrow morning. She put that note down and picked up another:

Chase last 3 photos for sticking on the gold stars

She found the list of invited people; a neat red line ran through all those whose photos were now stuck on the stars in the venue, strung with gold ribbons and ready for hanging. Three names didn't have a line through them. Name one: Charlotte Lau. No point in phoning her: she had said she wasn't coming. Leigh had already downloaded one of her own photos of Charlotte for her star. She felt sure Charlotte would be there somehow. The other two names: Zoe Anderson and Ben Mather. Both too shy to send a photo. She sighed, found the class contact list and reached for her phone.

"Leigh, you're not still working on prom, are you? Her stepdad was standing in the doorway carrying his black leather briefcase, a tall, lean figure in his City banker suit. Her own dad was a doctor. No pressure there, then.

Leigh sighed. "Where else would I be?"

"How's it going?"

"It would be better if I could have some peace to get on with this. I've got a lot to catch up on."

"Well, if you had been concentrating in French today, you wouldn't need to catch up. . . Your Mum told me you had detention."

"I *know*! Thanks for reminding me. But in case anyone hasn't noticed I'm trying to organize—"

"The best prom ever. We know, we know. But, it doesn't have to be perfect, Leigh. It's for people who want to have fun – it won't matter if a few things go wrong. You've done most of the work. Give yourself a break."

Leigh looked up at the photo of Dee in her Harvard sweatshirt on the mantelpiece and gritted her teeth. "And be known as the girl who organized the rubbish prom. No thanks. Dee always says detail is everything."

"Ah, well – Dee, she's not you."

"Oh, thanks very much. What are you saying? That Dee does everything better than me? Great. Thanks *so much* for the support."

"No, I'm not saying that. I know Dee's a perfectionist, but I sometimes think she lacks a . . . a perspective. On what's really important in life. You haven't done anything else but prom for weeks. You have lovely friends and Owen's a great boy. . ."

Leigh groaned. "Well that's just great. But I can do as good a job as Dee, if you would let me. Now *please* can I get on with this?"

"OK, OK." He held up his hands in defeat and disappeared into the kitchen.

Leigh surveyed the table again. She felt another wave of tension. Now, where was she?

Her phone rang in her hand, making her jump.

"Hello, Leigh? Guess what?"

"Charlotte! Hi. Please tell me you've called to say you've changed your mind and are coming to prom because quite honestly I don't have time to listen to anything else."

"What? Are you serious? I've done something exciting. And I wanted you to know."

"Are you coming to prom or not?" Leigh snapped.

"You know I'm not." Charlotte sounded hurt. "I did something about my music. I've been wanting to tell you for ages, but you've been so—"

"Charlotte, are you kidding me? I'm sitting in front of a pile of stuff and I'm starting to freak out about how much I've still got to do. You're not even coming and you want me to take time out to talk to you about your *music*?"

"Well, I thought you'd want to know, because it's important to me, but I guess the only thing that's important to you right now is yourself."

"It's not about me, it's about prom," Leigh practically yelled down the phone. Leigh heard the click as Charlotte hung up on her. She plonked the phone down on the largest spreadsheet and put her head in her hands for a minute, then took a deep breath and blinked tears from her eyes. She sat up straight, reaching for the photo list again.

She could do this. She just needed to focus. It was worth all this stress.

Everyone would thank her tomorrow.

CHAPTER 14

Alex

9.00 p.m.

Alex wished she hadn't gone to the film. It hadn't cheered her up; it had just fed into all her insecurities. Saying goodbye to Grace and Evan outside the cinema she had felt only loneliness – because *theirs* was the kind of relationship she wanted. *That* was the real thing. She knew it was stupid to mind that she didn't have a boyfriend to go to prom with tomorrow. She would be with her friends, but . . . well, it would have been nice.

She stared out of the bus window and saw Lindsay knocking at the door of a small red-brick terraced house. Wasn't that Kristyn's house? Hadn't she heard Kristyn telling Lindsay she was starting a new job tonight? Alex shrugged her shoulders as the bus moved on.

Five minutes later she was walking down her own street. It was still warm and her neighbour was mowing his lawn, filling the late evening air with the smell of newly cut grass. All the houses in her street had neat front gardens with hedges at the front and tidy lawns like his. She reached her white garden gate, waited for the tabby cat next door to stroll casually past her, tail arrogantly vertical as always, and swung the gate open.

She stopped, stared, then stared again trying to compute what was on her front lawn. Lying on the grass, spelled out in red roses in big letters, was one word: "PROM?"

"A promposal? Somebody wants to take me to prom?" Her heart was catching up with her brain and starting to pound. She looked around wildly. "I've got a PROMPOSAL?!" She wanted to dance on the grass singing at the top of her voice. *It has to be him*. She weighed up the evidence. He had been there in the art room when she had said she liked roses. He was the only one who had responded. He had said it was "good to know". She'd thought he was teasing her, but clearly he had really meant it! She laughed. And to think she'd been embarrassed about it. . . What a waste of emotion – he hadn't thought she was an idiot. He had gone out and bought these roses and made this perfect promposal. Chris! The boy she had had a crush on for ever – he had asked her. It couldn't be anyone else. She hadn't looked at any other boy at school. Only him.

She took out her phone to take a photo; she was never going to forget this moment. She took a lot of photos. Then she began to pick up the roses. She would put them in a big white vase in her room. She would think about Chris every time she looked at them. She was going to get a boyfriend at prom.

"Seriously embarrassing, isn't it?" Above her, Harry was hanging out of his bedroom window. He shook his head slowly from side to side. "That is one *lame* gesture."

"Shut up, Harry, and go away."

"You're right – better not to be spotted around the tragic crime scene." The window closed.

"Hey, wait! Harry!"

The window opened again. "What? And be quick about it because I've got my reputation to consider here."

"Did you see who. . .?"

Harry sighed. "Do you honestly think I'd keep it quiet if I knew who had done it? I would have gone global to out such a loser. I wanted to get rid of the evidence, but Mum wouldn't let me. Apparently it's – Harry made speech marks with his fingers – "'none of my business'."

Alex blushed at the thought of her mother seeing the roses. Never mind. It wasn't the end of the world. She braced herself as she went into the kitchen. Worse than she thought: her mum *and* dad were there. She didn't know why it was, but both your parents being pleased for you about something like this was *always* going to be a totally hideous experience.

Her mother gave her one of those knowing mother smiles. Alex managed to smile back; she just had to get through this and then she could be on her own in her room. And phone Grace.

"You see that I am the wisest of the wise among all mothers and I was right about you being a gorgeous girl and that it was only a matter of time. . ."

"OK, Mum! I get it. Thank you very much."

"Just saying . . . that's all. And who is the lucky boy?"

Alex flushed bright pink. "I don't know. You didn't see him, did you?"

Her dad shook his head. "No, the deed was done before we got back. *Quite* the romantic! *Sure* you don't have any idea?" His enquiring eyes scanned her face for clues.

"No. Not a clue. Must get these in water."

Her mother rummaged in the cupboard and produced the large white vase and handed it to her, still beaming. "Taking it to your room, are you?" She took a bite of wholemeal toast and jam.

Alex saw her chance as she filled the vase from the sink tap. "What happened to no carbs?" she murmured.

"Thank you very much, Sherlock," her mother

replied, cramming the remaining evidence into her mouth. "Now begone with you!"

Holding the vase carefully, Alex made her escape.

In her pale blue room she moved a pile of magazines to the floor and placed the roses on her white dressing table where she could see them from her bed. They whispered, "Chris likes you. Chris *really* likes you," every time she looked at them. She could still hear the hum of the lawnmower and the birds settling in the trees outside her window. Hanging on the wardrobe door was her prom dress. She got up from her bed, took it down and held it against herself. It had happened at last. This was it. Tomorrow night the boy she had fantasized about for so long was going take her into his arms and pull her close. He wanted to be with her; he had thought about what she had said about her favourite flower. She looked at them for the millionth time; this time they said loudly, "Chris is going to kiss you." Her heart pounded. Her big dream was coming true. She took out her phone to call Grace – but then put it back on her bedside table. The moment was too perfect; she wanted to savour it all by herself for a while. She hung her dress back on the wardrobe.

She looked at the time. 8.30 p.m. Why wasn't it later? She was never going to sleep tonight. Why wouldn't tomorrow come sooner?

She caught her reflection in the mirror.

Oh my god! She had thought she looked all right. But now! She needed to do that deep conditioning oil hair treatment, face pack, body scrub and moisturizing treatment, and make-up practice. She'd never have the time to do everything she needed to be ready on time. She grabbed a towel.

Got to get started.

CHAPTER 15

Grace

9.30 p.m.

"Grace! I didn't think I'd get to see you today."

Grace wrapped the dog's lead nervously round her hand; she wasn't looking forward to this. Her golden Labrador sniffed happily round their ankles as they stood by a low wall. The name "The Bay Tree" was discreetly lit above the door of the restaurant behind them. Fairy lights twinkled in the bay trees standing at intervals along the wall. There was an outside dining terrace where people sat at tables laid with white linen, crystal glass and silverware.

"Don't get me wrong – you've made my day, but wasn't it a bit of a risk? This restaurant is quite a walk from your house. And anyway, I'm seeing you tomorrow, right?" The tall, slim boy in chef's whites, looking at her through his ridiculously long eyelashes, knew her too well.

"Mum's talking to caterers for the after-prom party so I told her I would walk Boris. And I had to see you. I've got something to tell you, something you won't like – but *please* promise me you will listen to the end?"

The boy frowned, his dark brown eyes suddenly wary. Then he looked at Grace's anxious face and his expression softened. He reached out to hold her hand, his long fingers wrapped between hers. "OK. Go on. Did you talk to Evan?"

"Yes, I did. I told him that he shouldn't live his life as a lie any more – that he should come out and there should be no more pretend relationship between us."

"And what did he say?"

"You said you'd wait till I finish talking."

"OK. Sorry."

"He says he will – he's going to come out. But. . ."

The boy groaned.

Grace braced herself. "But he needs some more time."

"What?! You're kidding, Grace! I can't go to prom with you? It's what I've been living for. I thought we both had."

"It's only for a little bit longer, Jason. Then all this will be over."

"Yeah, but it's prom night *tomorrow*, Grace. I've waited so long for it – for us to be together, for everyone to know. How do you think it makes me feel that I'm such a big secret?"

Grace bit her lip. "I'm sorry, but I can't help my stupid mother and I can't let Evan down, not now."

"But you can let *me* down?"

Grace sighed. "You know it's not like that."

A voice from the kitchen called out, "Hey, Jason – these guinea fowl won't cook themselves, you know."

Jason turned to the door and yelled, "One minute!" He looked back at Grace. "I've got to go – never going to be a Michelin-starred chef if I lose this job."

"You won't. You're the best apprentice chef they've

had – they'd be mad to let you go."

Jason pulled her closer. "Hope you feel the same way."

She rested her head on his white jacket. "These last six months have been the best of my life," she sighed. "You think after we've waited all this time I'd let you go now?"

He took a deep breath. "So only a bit longer, then?"

She nodded.

"Still got your mother to deal with. They're hardly going to be thrilled that you're dating a chef. Not quite what they had in mind for Miss Oxbridge, is it? I live in a council house, my parents run a Jamaican food stall down the market, I didn't finish sixth-form college . . . not quite the doctor or banker they're hoping for."

"You left sixth-form college because you got an apprenticeship at the best restaurant in town!" Grace exclaimed indignantly. "And ever since I've known you you've wanted to cook. When you cooked for Tom's birthday it was the most delicious thing ever. I can taste it now – lime-and-coconut chicken, so fresh and zingy, everyone went mad for it. You could have gone to college; you aced your GCSEs last year. You're just lucky to know what you want and have the drive and ambition to go for it now. Unlike most of us who haven't got a clue what we want to be. You're the most committed and ambitious person I know." She stopped herself suddenly and grinned. "In fact, now I come to think of it, you and my mother have a lot in common."

"Maybe we will get on, then. If she likes ambitious – I'm her man. Certainly no one's going to stop me getting to where I want to be." He took Grace's face gently between his hands. "I'm proud of who I am. I'm not prepared to hide in the shadows much longer, Grace... I care about you too much. I'm proud of our relationship and I want to shout about it to the world..."

"Hey! Are you ever coming in?" The voice from the kitchen was more insistent.

She grasped his jacket. "So do I, Jason, more than anything. Please. Not much longer – then we can tell the world at last. Please. You know how hard it's going to be for Evan. Huge. If he needs more time ... *please*?"

Jason looked deep into her eyes, and her stomach did a flip, just as it did every time she really looked at him. "You are a very special girl, Grace – you know that? It drives me mad that you care so much about people, but it's part of why I'm so crazy about you. Why can't every girl be exactly like you?"

"Well, that might be a problem for me," she laughed.

He gently pulled her towards him and kissed her, the softest kiss – a kiss that Grace wished could go on for ever.

"Hey! Jason, are you ever getting back here?"

Grace reluctantly drew back. "You'd better go."

"I can't stand saying goodbye to you like this."

"Soon you won't have to. Soon this will all be over."

"Promise?"

Her mobile pinged and she jumped as if electrocuted, then glanced at the text and sighed. "Got to go or she's coming to look for me." She saw his soft brown eyes cloud over. "Please don't look at me like that, Jason."

Her phone started to ring and she turned away to attend to its jarring tone. She began walking back down the street.

"Yes, Mum. I'm sorry. Sorry. Yes, I'm on my way."

CHAPTER 16

Kristyn

9.45 p.m.

"You look very pale." Diana was frowning at her. "Look, it's nearly 9.45. Why don't you pop out for some fresh air? You've had to take masses of information since you arrived this evening. I know it's a lot to remember. Take five. I'll be here when you get back."

Outside Kristyn took some deep breaths. She shouldn't have come. All she wanted to do was to go to bed and cry. She thought about ringing Lindsay, but she wasn't exactly a sympathetic friend and she knew it would end up with her complaining about the history test and how unfair it was, and Kristyn didn't feel like listening to anyone else's problems tonight. Everyone's life seemed pretty sweet compared to hers.

Her dress was ruined.

And Jessie's pale face and pleading red eyes had made no difference.

Her mum had met her at the front door after Kristyn had raced home from the shoe shop. "Now, Kristyn, it was an accident. . ." She had held out her arms as if to stall her – but Kristyn had barged past and run straight upstairs to her room.

She looked at her wardrobe: her beautiful dress was gone.

"Where is it?" she had screeched. "Where *is* it?"

Jessie had appeared at the door. Over her arm she was carrying a pure white satin dress – except now it wasn't. Now it had a large, dirty, dark-brown coffee stain all down the front, the grounds soaked into the fabric like mud splashed on snow.

Kristyn grabbed it and gave a groan of horror.

"Kristyn, I'm so sorry, it's just that Fallon Fernandez

is coming in for a few days to have her hair done for a series of massive publicity shoots, and after we'd finished her hair today I just knew that the sparkle on the neckline of your dress would be perfect for the shot. . .

Kristyn raised her head slowly.

Jessie ran swiftly on while she still had a few seconds. "It was only going to take a few minutes – you wouldn't even have known – but that stupid, stupid junior knocked coffee all over it. Honestly, Kristyn, we tried everything but we couldn't get it out. I'm so, *so* sorry."

Kristyn stood up, shaking the dress in Jessie's face. "Do you know how long I worked for this dress. I mean *this* dress? Do you know how many early mornings I've got up, tables I've wiped, dishes I've washed?" The smart of Chris's jibes in the coffee bar came back to her. Tears were falling down her face now and she couldn't stop them.

"I know. I know!" Jessie's voice was agonized. "I'll buy you another dress, I promise. I'll pay you back every penny it cost!"

"You can't pay me back this dress!" Kristyn

screamed. "You know it was a one-off. You can never, *ever* pay me back for what you've done." She sat down on her bed and started to sob, thinking she would never be able to stop. This was a nightmare she couldn't wake up from – all that work, all that looking forward to wearing the dress, to looking good for once. Evan seeing her in it. People at school noticing her. All those dreams. All ruined. "I can't go to prom now," she choked, "I don't want to go to prom now."

Jessie burst into tears.

"Shut up! Shut up! I don't know why *you're* crying," Kristyn yelled. "It's not *your* life that's just been trashed. Why couldn't you let me have just one thing for myself? *Just one thing?* But no, you had to go and take away even that, didn't you? *Didn't you?*"

"Tomorrow," Jessie sobbed, "I'll take you shopping after work – we'll get you a wonderful dress."

"No, you won't," Kristyn said coldly. "I'm not going to prom, so forget your offer. Now if you don't mind I've got a new job starting today."

"Do you have to go, love?" her mum asked anxiously. "I don't think you should in this state."

"Yes, I do have to go, if I ever want to have money for anything else in my life. I do. And I can't stay under the same roof as *her* for another minute," she growled. "Now leave me alone." She chucked a file across the room. "Lindsay is going to come for this later this evening. Just give it to her."

She wasn't sure how she got herself ready for work and out of the house. She was glad her mum took the dress away; she couldn't look at it without bursting into fresh tears. All that time and effort – for nothing. And whatever dress Jessie could buy her in their town wasn't going to look like that one.

When she got to the restaurant she began to feel nervous. It wasn't anything like the coffee shop. There were bay trees outside in white wooden boxes with twinkling fairy lights. They welcomed you into the kind of place she had certainly never eaten in. Could she do this? The pay was good and the tips would be good too; everyone sitting at the tables looked wealthy. They had to be to eat here – the head chef was famous. Even so, she was relieved she would be working with another waitress – the older, smiling, grey-haired woman called Diana, who had let her take this break. Kristyn walked morosely out to the side of the restaurant and stopped dead. Grace was walking up the road.

Grace? What was she doing around here? Kristyn dipped behind one of the bay trees; the last person in the world she wanted to see tonight was Grace. Grace who had her wonderful brand-new designer dress safely at home and her gorgeous boyfriend: *her* prom was going to be perfect.

Someone was coming out through the restaurant door. It was one of the chefs, the one with a slight Jamaican accent. She'd met him when Diana had taken her around the kitchen. Jason. He was impossible not to notice, with his intelligent brown eyes and soft smiling mouth. Kind, too. When she saw him in the hectic restaurant kitchen he had bothered to take time out of his frantic work to wish her luck and tell her it was a great place, which had made her feel better.

She watched as he greeted Grace; Kristyn knew he had been at Harper High the previous year. Kristyn went very still, because she could see immediately, from the way they were talking and touching each other, that they knew each other well. What the hell was going on?

He had her face in his hands! But Grace had Evan. What was she doing with Jason? She couldn't be cheating on Evan. Could she? *Seriously?* Cheating on Evan! Why would anyone do that? If you have the best-looking, nicest boy in the school, what kind of hard-hearted, cold, mean person are you to cheat on him? Or wasn't Evan enough for Miss I-Have-to-Have-Everything? She just had to have more, didn't she? When some people had NOTHING. Kristyn's blood started to boil. She had had enough of selfish, thoughtless people. She got out her phone. Why should Grace get away with it? *Why should she have everything her way?*

Jason and Grace didn't notice her getting out her phone to take a picture of them as they kissed.

Kristyn put the phone back in her pocket.

She had the evidence.

Proof that Grace didn't deserve Evan.

Maybe he might look at someone else if he knew the truth.

Her heart gave a flicker of hope.

CHAPTER 17

Grace

6.45 a.m., the day of prom

"You *will* go." Grace's mother was standing at her bedroom door, dressed in a long pink silk dressing gown, her face thickly iced with a face pack.

Grace looked at her phone: it was 6.45 a.m. "But Mum, it's prom tonight – can't I have a lie-in just once?"

"Lie-in today, lie-in next week, soon it will be lie-ins every day. No, you're going to athletics training and that's that. It will give you a glow for tonight."

"I *have* a glow! A very expensive fake glow. Please, Mum, just *one* Saturday morning – *and* I was up late doing that maths project for my tutor."

"Tea, love?" Her father's kind face appeared around her mother's bony shoulder.

"She hasn't got time for tea in bed!" her mother snapped. "Take it downstairs and she can drink it on her way out."

Her dad sighed, turned and headed back downstairs.

Grace pulled her duvet over her head. "I'm not going."

Her mother ripped the duvet off her bed. "Oh yes you are. You are going because you are going to make the very best of yourself, my girl. You are going because you are *not* going to be just 'good enough' like some people I know. I want to be able to look our neighbours in the eye for once."

"Hey! Dad is not like that. He's always looked after us really well. You're just saying that because he didn't get that *one* job that you wanted to boast about to your so-called friends. You made him go for it and you knew he would have hated it."

Her mother's eyes flashed dangerously and Grace

knew she'd gone too far. "We'll never know, will we? But you – you will succeed; that is my one aim, my project."

"But don't you get it, Mum? I don't want to be your project, the thing you can boast to your friends about. I just want to be your . . . your . . . daughter."

"Don't be ridiculous – of course you're my daughter. Haven't I done everything to make this prom perfect for you?"

Grace's phone pinged. She frowned. Who else was awake at this time? She flicked a glance at what was on the screen and sat straight up. "You're right, Mum, you're right. I'm getting up – I'm getting up right this minute."

She scrambled across her bedroom, into her running vest, shorts and tracksuit and out of the house in what felt like minutes, watched by her triumphant mother.

Who thought she had won the argument.

If she only knew.

She texted Jason as soon as she was out of the house: "Meet me at the athletics track in an hour."

She had just finished a gruelling run when she looked up and saw him sitting on the spectator benches watching her. She jogged over.

"So what's the big deal?" he asked. "I was working till one o'clock this morning so it'd better be good to get me up this early on a Saturday."

She fished her phone out of her pocket and handed it to him.

He stared at the picture on the screen. "I really am one handsome dude, aren't I?" he grinned.

"Shut up, Jason!" Grace snatched the phone away. "It's not funny. There's a text that goes with it. . ."

"Who's it from?"

"I don't know. I don't recognize the number. The message begins, 'You lying cheat. I saw you. If you don't do what I tell you, this picture goes round the whole school.'"

"Nice. So what do they want you to do?"

"Says they'll text later today and let me know."

"So tell them to get stuffed. It's a pic of you and me kissing. So what?" He reached out to hold her hand.

She gasped, "'*So what?*' So Evan is totally humiliated just before prom? That's too mean. And remember our fake relationship has helped us too. My mum would never have let me out so often if she hadn't thought I was seeing Evan. We owe him. I *promised* him I'd give him longer. I can't go back on my word."

Jason pulled his hand out of hers and held both his arms away from her, above his head, as though he was suddenly allergic to her. "You just have to please everyone, don't you, Grace? Everyone except me."

"That's not true, Jason. But you have never, ever understood what it's like in my house, the pressure I'm under – the pressure that Evan is under, too. You just couldn't understand."

"Do you understand how that makes ME feel? I feel like your shameful secret. Mustn't let Grace's parents know about Jason: seems to me it quite suits you Evan wanting to keep his secret, not having to tell your mother about me. . . I'm beginning to think it's not just Evan that's stopping you."

Grace flushed. "That's not true!"

"Really? Seems that way to me, Grace."

"You think it's all so easy. Well, it is for you, with your parents who listen and trust you to make your own decisions in life – but it's not like that for everyone, you know. And it's not that easy to fight back."

"I don't see why not. You could if you really wanted

to," he said darkly.

A heavy silence fell, until Grace managed a weak protest: "You've never supported me in trying to protect Evan, trying to help him do the right thing in his own time and not before he's ready. . ."

Jason snorted, "Are you kidding? I've put up with being a ghost boyfriend for six months for Evan." He jumped down from the bench he was standing on. "Do you know? Forget it. I'm done. Either you text back to the mystery blackmailer and say 'Go ahead', or it's over between us."

"What! No, Jason, please!"

"Fine, then. I'm going. Enjoy your precious prom tonight. At least you'll never have to worry about your mother finding out about me. That'll be a massive relief for you."

She shouted after him as he walked away, "At least I care about my friends."

"Great!" she heard him yell. "Because that's all you're ever going have unless you learn to stand up to your mum."

She felt the tears coming as she looked back at her phone. This wasn't how things were supposed to be at all. Who could hate her enough to send that text? What did they want her to do?

She had a sudden urge to run after Jason. She stood up, looking wilding around her, trying to see which way he had gone.

"Grace! Grace! What are you doing?" Her mother's voice cut through the summer morning air as she stood waving at the track entrance. "I've got your maths tutor to come early so you have more time to get ready for violin practice. We need to go now!"

Grace sighed, pushing her phone into her pocket, and headed down towards the track.

"Who was that boy I saw walking away from you?" her mother asked. "I do hope he wasn't bothering you. I didn't like the look of him *at all*."

CHAPTER 18

Charlotte

9.00 a.m.

Charlotte had woken up in a foul mood.

She counted out the reasons on the kitten's paws.

Her best friend couldn't give her even a few minutes of her precious time on the phone; Leigh was too busy with stupid prom to pay any attention to Charlotte and her dreams. Leigh knew how important songwriting was to Charlotte, yet she had been so busy Charlotte hadn't even had a chance to tell her she'd entered a songwriting competition. Not that she'd got anywhere with it, Charlotte thought morosely, looking at her empty email inbox.

And on top of that there wasn't a single boy in the school she fancied and she didn't see how she was ever going to meet anyone anywhere else. Ever. And she was fed up with pretending she was too cool to care.

And tonight it was the blasted prom. Which she actually *was* too cool to care about.

As far as she could see, prom brought out the worst in everyone. She thought about the conversation she had overheard on the bus between Lexie and Lindsay.

Really the very worst.

But it was none of her business and she was sticking to her resolution to have nothing to do with it. Let them do whatever they wanted. It wasn't her problem.

Prom was nothing to do with her.

She heard her mum getting up and wondered if her mum wasn't a tiny bit glad Charlotte wasn't going tonight. They really didn't have masses of money for dresses and shoes and stuff.

Lucky Charlotte preferred vintage, anyway. She never stressed about what she was going to throw on in the morning; she just did it and somehow it came out right.

After a shower, she pulled on black skinny jeans, her black suede slouchy boots and a red top with a tiny white stars all over it; over the top she put on her short vintage denim jacket, then pulled her beret over her shiny bob. Some red lipstick, an expert flick of liner and mascara, and she was good to go.

Her mum smiled as she bumped into her coming out of her room. "Very Greenwich Village."

Charlotte grinned at her. "One day, Mum, one day."

When she was little they had lived in the Village, a boho part of Manhattan full of musicians and artists. She could only just remember its red-brick houses in tree-lined streets, with their tall steps up to the front doors and black fire escapes with pots of flowers on the edges. Her mum's eyes always grew softer when she talked about it. It was a place that reminded her of happy times with Charlotte's dad.

When she arrived at Vinyl Village, Charlotte waved to Cathy, the owner. Charlotte was grateful that Cathy had stopped asking her about the competition. Nothing had come in the post or her email this morning, either. She was going to have to forget it and deal with the disappointment. Cathy seemed to know Charlotte needed to be busy and asked her if she'd mind putting some new CDs in the racks. She started to put them in alphabetical order. It was a good way of checking out anything new in the shop, and for a while the rest of the world disappeared.

She swore she sensed the boy before she saw him.

She was standing by the racks, reading a CD cover, when the hairs on the back of her neck stirred as if someone had breathed very gently on it. She instinctively turned her face and found it half an inch away from a chest, a chest covered in a navy T-shirt with a silver eagle on it; it smelled newly washed and of . . . what? Boy?

She'd been physically close to boys hundreds of times, passing them in the corridors, sitting next to them at school. She'd never wanted to breathe one in before.

She sprang back, embarrassed by her closeness. "Sorry!"

"Hey, don't be. My fault. I just couldn't help noticing you were looking at the Human Animals CD."

She raised her eyes above the T-shirt, trying to regain some control, and found herself staring straight into a pair of light green eyes, proper smiling eyes, lined with thick dark lashes, eyes that creased as if they had been in the sun all their life. A straight nose, and a full mouth with even white teeth. His sun-streaked blond hair was pulled back into a topknot.

"I thought they weren't too well known over here."

"You're ... American," she managed to say. *Brilliant*, she thought to herself. *Well done, Charlotte. Just brilliant.*

"Yeah, from California. Love that beret – I mean, I hope you don't mind me saying." He blushed.

Was *he* looking as if he'd been caught off-guard too? Charlotte thought she must be imagining it. She gathered herself. "I've just started listening to them – I think they're great. But this is the first time I've seen the CD. Great cover. Love the apes-looking-at-humans-behind-bars image."

"Do you?" He smiled that smile that lit up the

room again and reached out. "May I?" His fingers touched hers as she gave him the CD and as his tanned arm brushed against hers she noticed the hairs on his forearms were bleached blond by the sun.

I mustn't be an idiot, she thought. "What other bands do you listen to?" she asked in a rush, filling the silence.

He smiled at her and she forgot to be nervous. Somehow it felt like the most natural thing in the world to be chatting to an American boy about music. She felt relief to be with someone who really understood what she was talking about, as if she had known him for years. And yet at the same time she was also experiencing a strange new sensation of adrenaline coursing through her bloodstream. She had never felt that before. No wonder Sleeping Beauty was woken with a kiss. Aaargh! What was she thinking? *Keep cool, Charlotte. Just keep cool.*

"Hey! Jackson, we've got to go. Now! Our ride's here!" A loud American voice cut through their conversation just as a large black van outside hooted its horn.

A smaller, dark-haired boy grabbed the blond boy's

arm and pulled his friend towards the street, smiling apologetically at Charlotte. "Sorry to break up the party, but we're gonna be late and that will NOT be cool."

Jackson turned round as he headed for the door. "I don't even know your name, Beret Girl, but I'm going to be at the Triangle tonight. Can you meet me there at 7.30? Please?"

She stood there, speechless.

He shook off his friend at the door and turned to look straight at her. "Please?"

She nodded and managed to say, "OK. Tonight. 7.30."

His face broke into a relieved smile. "Great. See you later, Beret Girl."

Her heart flipped over.

Forget prom.

She had something so, so much more exciting to look forward to.

She hugged her secret to herself and hummed the first bars of "Would You Know Me?"

CHAPTER 19

Alex

10.00 a.m.

"Honestly, Alex, it's not that bad."

"*Not that bad?* It's a disaster! Look at it." Alex tugged at her hair with both hands. The towel draped over her head fell on to the kitchen floor, exposing long, snake-like, greasy locks.

"Mmm . . . it is pretty bad, actually."

"Shut UP, Harry!"

Her mum picked up the towel and handed it back to her. "Alex, there's no need to worry, because you're going to the hairdresser's today and they will wash it out. It will be as if it never happened."

"How much olive oil did they tell you to put on?" Harry asked. "I may be out on a limb here, but I'm guessing you might have put a tiny bit more on than the magazine said. . ."

She glared at him, then answered tightly, "Perhaps a little."

"A little like a bucketful. You could fry enough chips for the school in that oil slick."

Her mum looked at her and Alex could see she was trying not to laugh. "Well, Alex, no one will be able to say that your hair isn't well nourished."

"I'm glad I'm providing so much amusement for you all. Very kind of you. Very kind indeed. And I'm worried the oil got on my face in the night and I'm going to get spots."

"You mean, more than you've got already?"

"Harry, you're a moron. I've got none, thank you very much, but I can feel one threatening on my chin. I've been on an anti-spot regime for months getting ready for this prom – you could operate off my face it's so clean."

"Unlike your pillowcase, I'll bet," said her mum. "Go and put it in the wash."

While Alex was upstairs the doorbell rang.

"The boy next door," her mum said as Alex came back down into the hall – to find Tom standing there. Tom caught her eye, and Alex grinned and rolled her eyes. Her mum said it without fail every time he came round. Which was often, as he was one of her best friends.

"What's with the Medusa look?" Tom grinned as he sat down at the kitchen table. Harry beamed at him. Tom, tall, athletic and on the swim team, was his hero.

"*Et tu, Brute*?" She sighed.

"She was trying to make a salad in her hair," Harry offered, "because she's had a promposal from some poor deluded boy. Who has a lettuce fetish."

"A promposal? That's news. Who from?" Tom asked, gratefully taking the cup of tea her mum handed to him.

"Some mystery admirer, but don't panic – the men in white coats are sure to pick him up soon. He won't be a danger to society for long."

Tom laughed.

"Harry! Come on, it's time for your football

practice." Mum was standing at the door holding a sports bag. "If you want a lift you've got sixty seconds or the offer is off the table. Dad's at the allotment and wants picking up."

Harry leapt up and they were gone.

Alex found herself blushing as she said, "It's going to look OK, you know – the hair, tonight."

Tom nodded. "That's good. I mean, not that it looks that terrible – I mean, your hair usually looks . . . er, fine."

"*'Fine'!* Is that the best you can do? Seriously, Tom, I have to look my best tonight. It's important because actually I do know who the promposal was from."

Tom leaned forward. "*Do* you? Who? I thought from what Harry said you didn't know."

"Ah, but I do." She wrapped the towel back round her head. "It's Chris."

"Chris!" Tom sounded genuinely surprised.

She turned on him, her cheeks flushed. "Yes, Chris – why sound so shocked? You think he wouldn't ask me? That I'm not good enough for him?"

Tom nearly choked on his tea. "No! No! It's just that I hadn't noticed him taking that much interest. . ."

Alex blushed an even deeper red. "Why would you? Boys don't notice stuff like that. Why would *you* notice who's looking at *me*? But he did – and do you know why?"

"Enlighten me."

"In art yesterday I said that red roses were my favourite flower."

"And?"

"*And* Chris heard me. He commented on it. Anyway, last night I came home and – TA-DAH! Roses saying 'PROM?' on the front lawn. What do you think of that, Sherlock?"

"I think that Chris is not usually known for his thoughtful and romantic gestures, that's what I think."

"Well, you never actually talk to him, do you – so what do you know? And I'm sure it's him. Who else could it be? He thought of this amazing way of asking me and now I'm feeling sick with terror because I know he's out of my league. . ."

Tom tipped his chair back. "Shut up! *Out of your league* – that has to be the biggest load of. . ."

"Come on, loads of girls like him. He's chosen me for now – but after tonight, when I actually get to go on another date with him, what about when he sees the real me? Not prom-dress, hair-done, glamorized Alex, but everyday. . ." she threw up her hands in horror and clutched Tom's arm. "Oh my god! What if he saw me like *this*?"

Tom grinned, showing his even, white smile. "You mean sitting-in-your-Paddington-onesie-with-hair-dripping-oil-down-your-face Alex."

She gave his arm a playful thwack. "Yes. That's what I mean. That's not the kind of girl he's going to like, is it? He must never, ever see me as I really am."

"What? You're a nutjob, Alex."

"I'm serious, Tom. You know all the girls he's been out with . . . they've all been a lot more. . ." She frowned and pulled the towel down over her face.

Tom's chair thudded back on all four legs as he leaned forward. "A lot more what?"

She buried her head completely in the towel and put her forehead on the table. "Experienced," she mumbled from underneath it. "And I know you're laughing. Stop it. I'm serious." She emerged from the towel to see Tom had obviously composed his features. "So what can I do, you know, to keep someone as amazing as Chris interested in a girl like me? I want him to think I'm cool – which I know I'm not. but you know what I mean. . ."

Tom pushed his dark brown fringe out of his face. "Well, don't show the slightest bit of interest in him as boyfriend material – that's always a winner."

"Too late for that – I've been staring at him all term in a notice-me way."

"I noticed."

She pulled the towel over her face again. "God, I'm such a dork. No wonder nobody asks me out."

Tom lifted the edge of her towel and watched a drip of oil fall off her nose. "You're very cool. It's Chris who's not cool."

"Well, I think sending a red-rose promposal is super-cool and I wouldn't have wanted any other boy to do it. He's the one, Tom."

"Is he?"

"He really and truly is."

"He's a jerk, Alex."

Her face fell. "Do you know, Tom" – her eyes flashed – "do you know how long I've liked him and looked forward to this? I get asked to prom by the boy

I really, really like and you're trashing it. Stop it. Be a good friend and be happy for me."

Tom scraped his chair back. "You're right, Alex – but good friends look out for each other too."

She pulled a face.

"I'm off now. Said I'd help out with getting the drinks in for tonight before swim meet. Wondered if you wanted to come – but I can see you're busy."

She reached out and grabbed his arm. "Chris really is amazing, you know, Tom. Can't you understand me being a bit scared? I've waited for this night for ages. . ."

"No. I won't understand you being a bit scared. Because he's not worth it."

She heard the door slam as he left.

Thanks for nothing, she thought; *thanks for a big fat nothing*. The first time she was getting what she wished for and Tom was trying to spoil it. "I don't care if he doesn't like Chris," she said to herself, getting up and rearranging her towel in a turban before starting to climb the stairs, "because I do."

She saw the roses on her dressing table and smiled.

CHAPTER 20

Grace

1.00 p.m.

It had been easy to get into the school.

The hall was full of workmen and she had slipped quickly past them through the corridors to Mrs Keane's office. No one had even noticed her, let alone asked what she was doing. That was the benefit of being a straight-A student – no one thought she could possibly be up to anything wrong.

Coming to a corner, she heard a loud girl's voice.

She moved quickly into a classroom and shut the door quietly.

"Yeah, Lexie, I passed. A breeze, thanks to Kristyn. No one noticed I had her notes under the papers. Madame was too busy getting her marking done and watching Jed sweat all over his test. But he passed too! Prom is going to be really great now he's coming. . ."

Grace ducked below the small glass window in the door as Lindsay sauntered past, her phone clamped to her ear.

"I'm off to the Style House now. Kristyn's there. Going to pretend I'm dropping in to tell her the good news about me going to prom – but really I want to try and get her sister to do my hair. Kristyn said she messed up her dress yesterday and so she kind of owes her, I reckon. Going to lean on her a bit more to ask her to do my hair too. She's so desperate for friends she'd do anything for me."

Grace waited a moment, then silently opened the door and carried on. She looked at her watch. Plenty of time before her appointment at the salon.

She tried the door to Mrs Keane's office. It was locked. It was always locked when no one was in there – but when she had been waiting to see the head about Oxford entrance with her parents, she had seen Miss Summerfield take a key from a hook behind her and open her top desk drawer. Grace found the first key and opened the drawer. She grabbed the key lying there – and a moment later found herself alone in the head's office.

She had to act fast.

The text with the instructions had come just after her maths tutorial. They were quite clear.

The ballot boxes were on the desk. One labelled "Prom King" and one "Prom Queen". She pulled down the second box and sank to the floor. She didn't want anyone passing to see her.

She opened the box and began to put the slips of paper inside into piles. When she had finished, she smiled sadly. Well, her mum would have been happy. Grace would have been Prom Queen. She was pleased to see that Alex had got a good few votes too, and Leigh. A wave of sadness came over her as she thought that it might actually have been fun to be Prom Queen. But then she pulled herself together. She didn't want Evan humiliated on prom night, and there was no need for him even to come out now. Jason wasn't her boyfriend any more. If Evan wanted to keep his secret a bit longer, he could. She no longer had anything to lose if they continued as they were.

Quickly, she began to write "Kristyn" on fresh slips and put them in the box. She took out just enough of the original slips so that Kristyn would have the highest number of votes. Then she threw the rest of the slips back in the box and shook it up. She put the box back on the desk, locked the door behind her, put the keys back and left.

Looking at Tom and Charlotte smiling through the Coffee House window on the way home had made her miss Jason. A huge ache inside her. She wondered if she could text him, ask him to see her. But what would be different? She couldn't let Evan down.

It had been a welcome distraction to help Alex get ready, but she had felt guilty too. Alex was her best friend, and she had never told her about Jason . . . because that would mean explaining about Evan. And Evan's secret wasn't hers to tell. She had wanted to tell Alex all about Jason about a million times; she had always shared everything with her. And today she had felt they had secrets from each other and she had hated that. She couldn't lose Alex as well as Jason.

Nothing was as it seemed. For her the whole evening would be a sham. She would see her friends arriving on the red carpet, all dressed up, even admiring her – but Evan wasn't her boyfriend and Jason didn't want to be with her any more.

Her life was lie. She felt trapped by secrets.

"Smile, darling!" Her mother had appeared at her bedroom door with a camera.

Grace turned her head and gave a huge smile.

My life is as fake as that photo, she thought.

CHAPTER 21

Leigh

2.00 p.m.

She wasn't at all sure that Charlotte would come to the salon.

Not after their phone call last night.

Leigh had texted her several times that morning but hadn't got a reply.

Even though she refused to come to prom, Charlotte had promised weeks ago to help her get ready on the day. Charlotte was a make-up genius; no one could do the black-eyeliner flick as perfectly as she could. But after yesterday, Leigh was convinced Charlotte wasn't going to turn up – and although she knew why, the selfish part of her was thinking that she had set the whole day aside to get ready and now she was going to have to do her make-up by herself. And as the organizer of the whole event, she needed to look perfect.

She scanned her list. She had had her tan done two days before so that was fine; she had a perfect golden glow now, just right to show off her dress. She looked down at it. It was royal blue, with a tight sequinned strapless bodice and a full net skirt – a real American prom dress: her mum and stepdad had had it sent over from New York. It had arrived in a huge box and when she had pulled it out and shaken the beautiful full skirts free from the white tissue paper, it was like all her birthdays rolled into one.

She turned her head from side to side in the salon mirror. Her long blonde hair had been up-styled in an elegant twist, with blue jewelled clips woven into it. She wasn't the only girl getting her hair done in her prom dress; no one wanted to pay Style House prices and then get their tiaras, bows and clips caught up in yards of material as they pulled an expensive dress over it.

Suddenly her eyes opened wide as a woman walked past her in the middle of an entourage of buzzing people. They were all dressed in black and in the centre of the group a tiny, curvy brunette dressed in a neon-yellow Versace jumpsuit, with hair cascading down her back, drifted by like an exotic flower. Leigh whispered to her manicurist, "Isn't that Fallon Fernandez? Isn't her album number one this week?"

The manicurist nodded, but didn't look up from carefully painting blue varnish on Leigh's perfect oval-shaped nails; she was used to celebrities in the salon. "She's come to finish being styled for that big hairspray promotion," she answered.

The star was seated with a flourish and was immediately fussed over by stylists, make-up artists and a woman Leigh guessed was her personal assistant from the fact she was permanently on the phone. Jessie, the salon's top stylist, was talking to her. To her surprise, she saw Kristyn sitting at the back of the salon, her chestnut hair glossy and expensively styled; she had obviously decided to change into her prom dress later as she was still wearing jeans. She was leaning back in a chair having her make-up done now, her hands draped over its white leather armrests. Leigh noticed her bright high-gloss red nails.

Lucky, lucky her, Leigh thought, remembering suddenly that Kristyn was Jessie's sister. She would have loved Jessie to do her hair, but Jessie was always booked up months ahead, and she was nearly double the price of the other stylists. Leigh watched, fascinated, as the door of the salon opened and someone wheeled in a rack of clothes. Not just any clothes – Leigh recognized Chanel labels on the evening dresses, as well as Dior, Versace and Vivienne Westwood. Someone was opening suitcases of accessories and it was like Aladdin's cave: boxes and boxes of jewellery, green, red and diamond stones and hair accessories. Now a nervous-looking man in huge black-rimmed glasses was wheeling in a rack of silk shoes in deep, vibrant yellows, pinks, blues, silver and gold.

She noticed Kristyn sitting up and watching too. Who wouldn't? Everything was gorgeous.

"Hello, loser. I have decided to forgive you for being the worst friend in the world."

She had been so engrossed she hadn't noticed that Charlotte had appeared at her side. "Charlotte! You're here! I'm so pleased," Leigh cried out with genuine emotion.

Charlotte moved in to give her a hug.

"Eek! Don't. My hair! My nails!"

The manicurist had finished now and indicated Charlotte could take her seat. Charlotte sighed and plonked her make-up bag on the ledge in front of the mirror.

"Have you seen Fallon Fernandez over there?" Leigh whispered.

"Mmm," Charlotte responded. "She's not really my type of artist. Too groomed and mainstream. And anyway, who cares about her? Haven't you got something to say to me?"

Leigh looked at her, puzzled.

Charlotte saw Leigh's blank face and exhaled slowly. "Like 'Sorry' and 'Thank you so much for coming in spite of my being so mean last night, you dear kind friend'?"

Leigh sighed. "I *am* sorry. I just couldn't talk last night, I had so much still to do. I was so stressed."

"Mmm. . . Well, I've got to be somewhere pretty cool myself this evening, so let's get on with it. I'm going to start with a primer now." She began to rub cream deftly into Leigh's forehead. "I want to say, though, that you know sometimes, just sometimes, friendship is more important than prom. Luckily for you, something good happened to me this morning – something really good, something *so much* better than prom – and I'm feeling forgiving."

But Leigh wasn't listening; she was distracted by Fallon shaking her head furiously at the stylist who obviously wasn't getting the combination of outfits right. How great to be that powerful, everyone hovering around you. Leigh sighed in admiration. And to get there by hard work and never settling for anything less than the best. Whatever the sacrifices.

"Leigh! Are you listening to me?"

Leigh nodded vaguely.

"No you're not! Now close your eyes – I'm going to do your liner now."

"Please make it perfect."

Charlotte gave an exasperated sigh. "Perfect. Perfect. Nothing is perfect, Leigh. That's why I hate prom –

it's all this fake 'It's going to be so wonderful' thing."

"It *is* going to be wonderful."

There was silence for a while as Charlotte's brushes did their magic. Then she stepped back to look at her work and said, "Not for everyone it isn't."

"What do you mean by that?"

Charlotte shrugged her shoulders.

"No," Leigh insisted as Charlotte brushed blusher on her cheekbones. "Tell me. What do you mean by that?"

"Just that prom is fine if you are Miss Preppy Popular, but for other people, perhaps for less confident people, it's an evening that highlights all their insecurities and it makes them feel the opposite of good about themselves. How can that be a good thing?"

"What are you on about? Everyone is going to have an amazing time. I've arranged everything!"

"You can't arrange *everything*. You're not God. Now stop moving; the liner will smudge."

"Name me one thing I've forgotten – one thing. Honestly, this makes me mad when I think of all the last-minute changes I've had to deal with. . . You . . . you've been so selfish you don't even care what's happened to cause so much last-minute panic and work."

"Me! Selfish?"

"Yes, you. This matters to me so much; I've had to deal with a major crisis with the caterers and you've done nothing but trash all the work I've done. I call that selfish when you're supposed to be my best friend."

"What! You won't speak to me on the phone, yet I still come here to do your—" Charlotte paused, the blusher in mid-air. "Do you know? Forget it. Talking to you I've just realized I've got better things to do. Do your own make-up." She threw tubes, mascara, eyeliner and various compacts into her bag and stormed out.

Before Leigh could even register the stares of everyone in the salon, her phone rang.

It was the prom venue. A voice droned in her ear, "The girl you sent over has had to go, so she can't finish hanging all the stars but there are only ten of them left. Maybe you can give them out at the end—"

Leigh wailed. "We can't not have *all* the stars hung – it just won't be completely right." She looked at her reflection. Charlotte had finished the hardest part; she could manage the rest later. "Look, I'll do it myself. I'll be over as soon as I've finished some things at home."

She looked down at her long, full net skirts and matching blue satin heels. Not quite the right outfit for climbing ladders – but those stars had to hang.

Of course Charlotte would say it didn't matter.

But it did matter; it mattered to her.

CHAPTER 22

Charlotte

2.30 p.m.

As Charlotte left the Style House, bag flying, she crashed straight into Lindsay, who was yelling to the whole street, "I'm going to prom!"

Charlotte's make-up scattered over the pavement.

Lindsay yelled to the sky, "I aced that history test and I'm going to prom!"

Charlotte swooped to save an expensive lipstick from disappearing under Lindsay's foot.

"How on earth did you pass, Lindsay?" Charlotte snapped as she stood up. "Cheated, I expect."

Lindsay reared back in mock horror. "Ooh, harsh words. And anyway, what are you doing here? I thought you were too stuck up your own beret for prom."

"I'm ... I was ... oh, never mind. Jed said he'd been working pretty hard – did he pass?"

Lindsay's eyes narrowed. "Yes, he did – and what's it to you? It's not as if he's interested in you."

Charlotte threw back her head and burst out laughing. Lindsay growled, pushed past her and disappeared into the salon.

Her phone pinged. It was a text from Tom: "We can see you across the street from the Coffee House. Just finished a swim training session. Come and join us."

Charlotte got on well with most of the boys in her year, especially Tom, who was one of the good ones. She thought about it for a moment ... she needed to get ready for tonight – but her truncated visit to Leigh had given her some extra time.

She walked into the café, and Evan and Ben moved up the red leather seat on one side of the booth to make room for her. She looked around: Chris, Tom, Evan and Ben. No one could deny that all that exercise and gym work had reaped benefits. If only Ben wouldn't wear those awful massive T-shirts and baggy old trousers. He was, it had to be said, a style disaster. She even saw a glimpse of shark's-tooth necklace. Oh dear.

"Still haven't changed your mind about tonight?" Chris said, stretching his tanned muscled arms high above his head for her benefit. Out of all the boys in the team, Charlotte found Chris the hardest to get on with. There was no doubt he was capable of deep love and affection, but it was a pity it was only for himself.

She shook her head. "Have you asked anyone?"

"Aah," he smirked, and Charlotte couldn't help noticing that his chin was rather weak, and his eyes might be deep blue but they could take on a weasel-like expression sometimes. Like now. "Now that would be telling, wouldn't it? Let's just say I'm keeping my options open for tonight. Haven't made up my mind who the lucky girl will be yet."

"Excuse me a moment while I puke," Charlotte answered coldly.

Tom gave a short bark of laughter and grinned at her. She grinned back; she guessed someone as bright as Tom would know Chris was an idiot.

"What's up with you, mate?" Chris asked, slapping Tom on the back. "Don't be jealous of the man. You could have asked a load of girls – I don't get it. Why didn't you, when you could have had your pick?"

Charlotte was about to lay into Chris for his medieval attitude – but Tom got there first. "Maybe it's because I see girls as, you know . . . actual human beings, really quite like us and, you know, not . . . not . . . interchangeable dolls. And the one I maybe want to go with isn't, er. . ."

"Yeah," Evan suddenly interjected. He had been sitting quietly, biting his nails, and Charlotte had felt the seat move as he jiggled his leg nervously. She wondered why he seemed so edgy. Nervous about prom? Hardly. "I think the word is 'respect'," Evan blurted out. "You know, Chris, people aren't toys you can pick up, play with and chuck out."

"The girls I know are." Chris raised his eyebrows

at Charlotte, who was wishing she hadn't come – but also knew there was no way she was going to let that statement go.

She leaned across the table. "That's because they are young and insecure and you're full of way, *way* too much misguided confidence, which they incorrectly interpret as some kind of strength of character. But you know something? All those girls, they're all going to grow up, and then boys like you won't stand a chance with them because they'll know what they're worth and it's certainly more than being messed about by someone who's too immature to care about anyone but himself. And then where will you be?"

Chris leaned back on the leather booth wall behind him, faking a relaxed attitude which she could see he didn't really feel. His eyes darted from side to side at the others before narrowing at her. "What's eating you today with this feminist, lezzie stuff? What's with the women's-lib rant? You gone gay or something?"

"She's right," Evan said quietly. "I mean, about not seeing a girl as some kind of trophy beside you but seeing her as who she is, thinking about *her* feelings."

Everyone turned to look at him.

Chris gave a harsh laugh. "What? You going gay too?" Evan's shocked expression made Chris laugh again, and he leaned over and mussed Evan's hair. "Not with that gorgeous girlfriend, I don't think. Anyway, I reckon I'm on a dead cert tonight – she's been making it obvious all term. Pretty little thing she is, too. I'll leave the rest of you to your sad, lonely lives. Jealousy is a terrible thing, you know. Laters, guys!" He grabbed his bag and left, swinging the café door behind him.

"It's heartening to think how far mankind has come since caveman times." Tom shook his head.

"I think he left his club behind."

"Do you know if he *has* asked anyone to prom?" Evan asked.

"He's not saying," Tom answered, "but I expect he's got his eye on someone."

"And she'll fall into his arms," Ben sighed.

Tom grabbed his arm. "Come on, Ben, man up. You've got to ask her out sometime. When could be a better time than today? I'm telling you she likes you."

Ben blushed a postbox red, vehemently shaking his

head from side to side. "You don't know that. Why would she? I just can't do it."

Tom left it. Ben was clever but he was the most socially awkward boy in the year. It was hard to see him ever finding the nerve to talk to a girl on his own, let alone ask one out. Even with the other boys around today he could barely look at Charlotte. Tom patted him on the shoulder. "That's OK, man, forget it. We'll have a great time without dates."

Evan's phone suddenly pinged. Grabbing it to read the text, he accidentally knocked his coffee over with his elbow. He dabbed at the spill once or twice with a napkin, then said he had to get going. Charlotte frowned. What on earth was making him so jumpy today?

Ben said he had to be off too.

Charlotte was now left with Tom, which was what she wanted. She looked at her watch. She had her own dream boy to get ready for. But before that she had a couple of other things to do. "Tom," she began, "now the others have gone, can I ask you do something for me?"

"Sounds mysterious. What?"

"It's about prom."

Tom raised his eyebrows. "Really? I thought you hated prom and everything about it. Have you changed your mind? Fancy your chances with Chris?"

She smiled. "No to both those questions. I certainly won't be anywhere near it tonight. But there are some things I've got to do and I need your help."

Tom leaned back and folded his arms, "Sounds mysterious. OK then, let's hear it."

CHAPTER 23

Leigh

4.40 p.m.

If she hadn't been so tired it would never have happened.

If she could have been bothered to climb down the ladder and move it *right* under the ceiling hook, the hook where the very last gold star needed to hang, she wouldn't now be looking up at that star, waving on its gold string, from a horizontal position on her back on the floor.

Charlotte's star! The irony.

She had genuinely believed she could reach that last hook from where she had hung Zoe's star (photo emailed just in time, thank goodness). If she leaned over she persuaded herself she could just get at the hook without too much of a stretch; it didn't seem a crazy idea. As she leaned over, just as she finished tying the string, she had felt the slippery new soles of her blue satin sandals slip on the metal stepladder and then, very, very slowly, as if in slow motion, she had sensed that she and the ladder were going in different directions. Charlotte's face had looked on as she drifted past and then crashed down, the ladder smashing down next to her, bouncing with a metallic clang on the wooden floor.

She lay completely still, knowing pain would kick in the moment she moved. Surely someone would have heard the crash? But the room was empty and she realized no one was due to come for hours. She'd had to beg the doorman to let her have the key, promising she would hand it over to the evening staff. She rolled over and winced. Her wrist was agony. She must have tried to break her fall with her hands. Very carefully she managed to sit up. She gasped – her dress was ripped up one side; even the thought that it must have caught on the ladder and the rip had probably slowed her fall did nothing to comfort her. Her beautiful blue prom dress, ruined. She noticed blue sequins scattered on the floor around her.

As she reached for her bag, which was lying a few metres away, a bolt of pain shot through her body. She had taken the bag up the ladder to keep the string and scissors in, and when she fell the contents had scattered everywhere. Gingerly she shuffled her rear across the floor and hooked it towards her with her foot. She felt another stab of pain.

She groaned as she pulled her phone out of the bag. The screen was smashed. She pressed the power button, hoping that it would somehow still work – and to her relief, the screen lit up.

She punched in her mum's number but as soon as it started ringing, her phone powered off. She wailed in distress.

She tried Owen. "It's ringing! Please keep ringing, *please* keep ringing," she pleaded to it.

The phone obeyed. "Hi, Owen here – can't answer right now. Leave a message and I'll catch you later."

Where was he? Owen always answered his phone. She felt that wave of unease again. Was he still angry with her? Had she gone too far, taken his good nature to breaking point? The phone cut off again before she had even left a message. She switched it on again, deciding to try to send a text. She jabbed, "HELP!" and pressed "Send". The phone cut out while the message was still sending, and no matter how many times she tried the power button it wouldn't turn back on.

No one was coming. She needed a plan.

She needed to get to a doctor.

Her dad worked in Accident and Emergency and she knew where it was – only about twenty minutes' walk away. Could she hobble there and get seen quickly? Then she could still be in time for prom. Everyone else should know what they needed to do to set up the catering and entertainment. All the decorating was done – even Charlotte's star, thanks to her. They had needles and stitching stuff in hospitals, didn't they? She could sort her dress out while she was there.

She began to push herself with one arm to her feet. Her head spun and she felt very woozy. She really wanted to lie down on the floor again and go to sleep, but she knew she had to get moving. Once up, she leaned against the wall, testing her feet. One was sore, but not in agony like her wrist, and the other seemed OK. Holding her fragile arm with her other hand, she followed the wall to the exit and opened the door. Rain had just started to fall from the huge black clouds rumbling above her. She shrank back into the building. Her hair! Her dress! They'd be completely ruined by the rain. But she had no choice. She stepped forward and cringed as the first cold drop hit the tip of her nose.

She would get back to prom.

Why had she had to hang up that last star? As the rain soaked through her hair and her dress, she put one foot in front of the other and thought about it.

It would keep her mind off the pain.

She already knew the answer. She had wanted to put it up because she wanted Charlotte to be there, in some way. Even if it was only in the form of a photo on a gold glittery star hanging from the ceiling. Nothing was quite as much fun without Charlotte there. Charlotte, who had come to do her make-up even though Leigh had been so horrible to her on the phone the night before. She wondered what Charlotte's evening was going to be. She had been so excited about it at the salon – and Leigh hadn't even bothered to give her a few minutes to be heard.

And Owen . . . how she wanted to see him, and now he wasn't there for her either. Like Charlotte, he had tried and tried to get a tiny bit of her attention. Now she needed both of them and they weren't there. And it served her right. She thought of all the warnings they had given to show her they felt neglected. She stopped walking for a moment. Where was she?

What would happen at prom without her? She caught herself.

What had her stepdad said about Dee? He had been warning her too. But she had been too blind to recognize it, too busy focusing on her endless plans and lists. She realized that in all her timetables and to-do lists she had missed out time for the most important item of all. The people she cared about. And who cared about her now?

No one.

And it was all her fault.

CHAPTER 24

Kristyn

6.00 p.m.

She sat on her bed waiting for the doorbell to ring.

She thought back to early that morning. The house had been quiet and she had been lying in bed, thinking, her mind churning with what she had seen at the restaurant the night before.

Prom was all over for her. She hadn't even been going to get out of bed.

But there had been a tap on her door, and she had heard it open.

"Kristyn?" Jessie had whispered.

Kristyn hadn't moved under the duvet. She heard Jessie put a cup down on her bedside table.

"Kristyn, listen to me – I know you say I can't do anything to make it up to you about the dress, but I can do this; all the people in the salon want to help. Look, if we go in early, I can do your hair before the salon opens officially, then Shanique who does make-up says she can fit you in for a session – and so can Li who does manicures. Honestly, they're the best, Kristyn; we will make you look incredible, I mean really like a film star. It is a Hollywood Nights prom. There won't be a boy there who won't want to be with you. We're giving you something that would normally cost hundreds of pounds. There'll be no girl to touch you."

Kristyn had stirred under the covers. She was processing what her sister had just offered her. Perhaps this was her chance at last? Perhaps Evan, when he realized how two-faced Grace was, would see her at prom and he might, *at last*, see that she was the girl for him.

She had poked her head over the duvet and given

Jessie a level stare. "What about the dress – and shoes?"

"Mum says she could perhaps take you shopping after we've finished with you at the salon."

Jessie saw Kristyn's face tense.

"Honestly, Kristyn, you will look so stunning no one will seriously notice your dress. I promise, you will look like a princess."

Kristyn sat up.

Or a Prom Queen.

Evan was going to be Prom King. Everyone knew that.

Then she had known exactly what to ask Grace to do. It was all so simple. Her being at the restaurant last night was meant to be. Fate had given Kristyn this opportunity – and why shouldn't it be looking after *her* for a change?

"OK," she had said to an anxious-looking Jessie, whose tense face immediately broke into a broad smile. "Give me twenty minutes to get ready."

Jessie had rushed up to her and given her a hug, which took her by surprise. She couldn't remember Jessie ever hugging her before. Certainly not since they were little girls. It hadn't been so bad.

*

She'd sent Grace the instructions when she got to the salon. This time she hadn't hidden who she was. Grace was hardly going to tell anyone, was she?

And she had sent one to Evan too:

> I know something to do with you. Come over so we can talk about it.

She had wished she could be nicer, but she wanted to prepare him for what she had to say.

Evan had replied, saying he would come to her house at 6.00 p.m.

And now it was 6.05 p.m.

The doorbell rang and she jumped up.

She was grateful Jessie was still at work and her mum was watching TV in the sitting room as she opened the door.

Evan stared at her, obviously taken aback. "Wow, Kristyn," he said. "You look great."

Her heart sang. Evan was standing at her front door, telling her she looked great. "Thanks, Evan." She gave him her biggest smile. But he didn't look the way she thought he was going to when she had fantasized about this in the salon. His normally bright blue eyes looked dark and guarded and his usually friendly face had a hard look. Of course, he was anxious about her message. But it was better he knew the truth. She was doing the right thing. She was sure. "Do you want to come in?" She pulled the long red satin skirt of her dress to one side.

"No thanks," he said firmly. "Just want to know what you meant by that text."

She didn't recognize his voice. It was brusque and cold. She tried to keep her own voice calm, but found it was trembling. "I've found something out, Evan. And as your friend. . ."

She saw him flinch and her increasing level of anxiety shot up further. "As your friend, I think you should know about it."

Evan steadied his hand on the door frame. "And what would 'it' be, Kristyn?"

None of this was going to plan. She needed to tell him quickly and then he would understand. "Grace is cheating on you." She took out the mobile and brandished the photo. "Look – I saw her with another guy yesterday."

At first she imagined he actually seemed relieved at what she'd said. But then he slid his eyes away from the image and gave her a long, uncomfortable stare. "And this is your business how?"

She was shocked. This wasn't the plan at all. "Because I care about . . . about your feelings – and if it was me I'd really want to know if someone was making a fool out of me."

"Would you?"

"Yes! Yes, I would. She's making you look an idiot and I just couldn't bear the thought of seeing you at prom and you not knowing. I've told her as much too."

"But I know about Grace and Jason," he said calmly.

Kristyn thought she must have misunderstood. "What?"

"I know. I know about Jason and Grace."

"You know!" She stepped back in shock. "How long have you known? I bet she only just told you today because she knew she'd been caught in the act."

Evan leaned towards her. "I just know, that's all."

Kristyn was feeling like Alice in Wonderland when the whole pack of cards comes crashing down on her as she wakes from her dream. "I don't . . . I just don't understand. . ."

Evan was still glaring at her with that strange expression she couldn't interpret. "No, you don't. You have absolutely no idea what you're doing, do you?"

"I only wanted to help. . ." she spluttered.

'Well, if you think you are helping me, you aren't. You're doing the opposite. The total opposite."

Kristyn stood there and shook her head dumbly. She didn't understand. She had no idea what he was talking about. If he could just calm down and let her talk to him properly, then she could make him see that what she had done was the right thing. See that she cared about him and acted because she wanted him to be with someone who really appreciated him.

She gathered herself. "I don't understand, Evan. You already knew about Jason and Grace? So why are you still with her?"

He gazed at her, then took a deep sigh. "OK. Here we go. You going to let me in?"

Her heart skipped as she let him in. Perhaps it wasn't too late. Perhaps she could make him see that there were people who really cared about him and would never hurt him.

Maybe her prom-night dream could still be saved.

CHAPTER 25

Alex

6.05 p.m.

"Again?" Alex sighed.

"Again."

She peered at herself in the large mirror in Grace's bedroom. Grace was frowning over her shoulder.

"I think one more time and we'll be there, Alex. Come on, let's do it."

Alex stood up and headed for the basin in Grace's spotless white en-suite bathroom. "You're so lucky," she sighed. "How amazing not having to share your space with your brother's dirty socks, smelly T-shirts and open toothpaste tubes ... and don't even *talk* about the loo."

Grace winced.

"I know," Alex continued, "disgusting but true. But such is my life." She looked closely at Grace. "I'm sorry – I shouldn't complain; I haven't been up since first light running around tracks and then having hours of maths."

Grace had immediately offered to save Alex when the hairdresser had taken one look at her hair and refused to help because of the time it would take. However, Grace had seemed very distracted since she arrived and Alex wondered if the Prom Queen pressure was making her nervous. Well, if *she* was nervous she wasn't the only one. Alex had to look her best tonight. Even though Chris had already shown with the promposal that he wanted her to be his date for tonight, he could still change his mind when he set eyes on her. And for that reason she had decided to keep his promposal a secret. The thought of Chris changing his mind sent her into a tailspin of anxiety – she was glad her head was stuck in the sink under the shower fixture and Grace couldn't see her face.

She couldn't understand why Grace was so jumpy. She looked stunning. Her blonde hair was swept up glamorously and her perfect complexion hardly needed make-up. With her cream and gold lace dress, she looked exactly like a *Vogue* cover. To be honest, she still looked like one in her sweats, which was what she was wearing to wash Alex's hair. Typical Grace, fresh from the salon, not to mind getting out of her dress and potentially mucking up her make-up in order to help Alex.

"If you change your mind about Oxford you can always be a saint, or a model," Alex had told her when she turned up at her door, her hair still wrapped in a towel. "You look so lovely. Evan is going to be the happiest man at prom tonight."

To her surprise Grace had responded with nothing but a tight smile. It was as if Grace didn't want to talk about prom. Which actually was just as well since she herself didn't either, the Chris thing had sent her into such a whirlwind of self-doubt. He was so confident, so cool. What did he see in her?

How could she ever keep a boy like that interested in someone like her?

Grace finished Alex's fifth hair wash, put another fresh towel round her head (that was another thing about Grace's bathroom – endless clean white towels, all stacked up on white wooden shelves) and sat her back on the white chair in front of the mirror.

"I can't thank you enough for this," Alex said with feeling. "You have saved my life."

"You don't have to thank me. That's what friends are for. Don't worry." Grace picked up a strand of hair. "Success! The oil is totally out and you're good to go. Pass me the mousse and the big rollers." Alex handed them to her and Grace curled up a long strand of her hair and tucked it neatly into place.

"Anything on your mind, Grace?" Alex ventured.

Grace managed a laugh. "No. Guess I'm nervous about tonight. My mum's gone into overdrive; she's threatened to turn up for the crowning of the Prom King and Queen. So as not to miss the moment. . ."

"But parents aren't invited."

"You try telling *her* that. She's even mentioned wearing her old Prom Queen dress. I've asked her what's going to happen if I'm not Prom Queen but she won't listen."

Alex sympathized deeply with the thought of that horror – but she knew her friend and she knew she was hiding something else from her.

It seemed this prom was full of secrets for both of them.

"Guess what? Guess what Evan told me," Grace said.

OK, Miss Mysterious, I know you're just trying to divert me from your jumpiness, Alex thought to herself. "Go on," she said aloud.

"Evan says he thinks Tom is really keen on someone at school."

If she had wanted to divert Alex's attention she had succeeded. "What? Tom? No, that's rubbish. I saw him this morning. He never said anything."

"That's just it. He hasn't said anything to anyone, but Evan knows him pretty well and says he's just got this feeling from little bits that Tom's let out that he had hoped he might get together with someone at prom but she's not coming or something."

Alex handed Grace another strand of her hair.

"Evan says he's got a good idea who it is, too."

Alex was all ears now. "Who?"

"Charlotte Lau. And I saw them together in the Coffee House today when I came out of the salon, chatting away and looking very cosy I must say."

"Charlotte!" Alex was confused. Why hadn't Tom told her? Tom was supposed to be her friend, wasn't he? One of her best friends. He hadn't once mentioned being interested in Charlotte even when she had told him all about Chris. She felt a rush of anger. And what had he done when she told him Chris had shown serious interest at last? Been totally negative and tried to ruin the best thing that had ever happened to her. Maybe she had been kidding herself that she and Tom were such good mates.

"What do you think about that?" Grace continued. "I think they'd make a really cool couple."

"But she's totally anti-prom. She's not even coming!"

"I know. That's why Evan thinks Tom's a bit low about tonight. But it doesn't mean it's never going to happen, ever. Just because it doesn't happen at prom."

"Suppose so." In truth, Alex did think Tom

and Charlotte would make a cool couple. She was certainly smart, funny and clever enough for him. Did that mean he'd be sharing stuff with her from now on? From what Grace said maybe that had started already.

"They would be good together, wouldn't they?"

"Mmm. . ." Alex was still trying to overcome her bewilderment and irritation. Tom hadn't said anything to her and she thought they talked about everything. Maybe he had someone else to share stuff with now. That hurt.

"You OK, Alex?" Grace was getting out her make-up now.

Alex nodded.

"OK, close your eyes."

She obeyed.

Half an hour later she was standing in front of the full-length mirror on Grace's wardrobe, ready for prom.

"You look gorgeous, Alex."

She looked at her reflection. Her hair was elegantly swept back from her face with a pink ribbon and silver clips and then fell down her back in shining soft waves. Her make-up was perfect, the soft pink lipstick and blusher matching her dress, the grey eyeshadow and eyeliner making the green of her eyes stand out. The pearl earrings dropped delicately from her ears and her nails were perfect pink ovals with a crystal on each one, matching those on her dress. She reached out and grasped Grace's hand as she stood beside Alex in her cream-and-gold dress, her blonde hair, her make-up and nails immaculate. "Thank you, Grace. You've worked a miracle."

"Promise me I'm not going to have to tell you to stop putting yourself down tonight, then."

"Not tonight. I feel amazing."

"Good. Now, Cinderella, you must go to the ball."

The doorbell rang.

Grace jumped. "That'll be Evan in the limo. I'll get it." She dashed from the room.

Alex took a deep breath. Tonight was going to be her night – and nothing, nothing was going to spoil it. This was her chance with Chris; that was all that mattered. This was going to be the start of the rest of her life. The real life, the confident life of going out with someone she had dreamed about for such a long time – five whole years.

She blushed at her image in the mirror. Tonight, she hoped, she was going to have her first kiss.

The doorbell rang again. She could hear Chris's voice downstairs.

Everything was going to be different from now on. No more putting herself down. After all, she was going to be Chris's girlfriend after tonight. And everything would be like it was in the films she loved.

"The limo's leaving in ten minutes!" Evan yelled up the stairs. "It's prom time!"

Alex turned towards the stairs and gave herself one last glance in the mirror.

She was ready.

CHAPTER 26

Kristyn

6.10 p.m.

Kristyn's heart was pounding as she closed the door. Evan was actually in her house.

Now she could make him see that she hadn't taken that photo to hurt him. Make him understand.

"Where do you want to talk?" he asked brusquely, looking around the hallway.

She felt flustered. Not in her room – too personal. "Through here," she said, opening the door to the kitchen and firmly closing the door to the sitting-room where the TV was murmuring.

Evan sat down at the kitchen table. She could hardly believe this was happening. He looked so handsome; the ends of his dark blond hair were still damp from swimming and his tight-fitting white shirt showed off his broad shoulders. She tried to calm down – but Evan's black Levi's were sitting at her kitchen table. She thought of sitting next to him – too close, maybe; she changed her mind and sat down on the chair opposite.

"Who's there, Kristyn?" her mother called out.

"Just a friend, Mum – won't be long."

"Who?"

"Just a *friend*, Mum." *Please, please don't come in,* she thought to herself. *Please leave us alone.*

"Look, Kristyn—" Evan began.

"No, let me say this first, Evan." She wasn't going to mess up this one and only chance. "I took the photo because ... because I think you are a really nice person. I've always thought that about you. And when I saw Grace cheating on you I felt so angry, because . . . how could she?" She could see him staring at her now, but she couldn't read his expression. "You deserve a girl who appreciates you. Not one who makes a fool of you behind your back. But a girl who would never, ever cheat on you. . ."

"Like you, you mean?" Evan looked as though he was just starting to solve a puzzle.

She blushed furiously and turned her eyes away from his gaze. "No, that's not what I mean."

"So what is this all about? You wanted to break Grace and me up?"

"No – I just thought nobody should be with someone who's cheating on them. But now you say you knew about it. Surely you can't want to carry on with Grace knowing that? She's treated you so horribly badly. She's a cheat, Evan."

Evan put his head in his hands. "No, she's not. You don't understand – she's been the best, most loyal person to me in the world."

"You're right, I *don't* understand—"

He groaned and took a deep breath, looking up at her. "Grace has been going out with Jason for six months. She's only been pretending to go out with me – she's never been my girlfriend."

Kristyn opened her mouth but shut it again.

"It's true she's kept a secret from everyone else, but the real secret is that *our* relationship is fake. Her real relationship has always been with Jason. I am not, nor have ever been, Grace's boyfriend," he sighed, "nor ever will be."

Kristyn felt a flicker of hope.

Evan sensed it and shook his head. "You don't get it. I won't be *any* girl's boyfriend. Ever."

"I don't understand. . ." Kristyn insisted. "Why. . .?"

"Why do you think? Why would a boy *pretend* to have a girlfriend? And what reason would a boy have for saying he knows for sure he's never going to go out with a girl? Come on, Kristyn, you're smart. I'm sure I don't have to spell it out for you."

"Hello, dear – aren't you going to introduce me to your friend?" Her mother appeared smiling at the door. "Are you going to prom together? Doesn't Kristyn look lovely?"

"No! *Mum*, please, could we have a minute?"

Evan scraped his chair back. "I'm just going, actually. I've got to get dressed for prom – the limo's picking me up soonish. Nice to meet you, Mrs O'Malley."

Kristyn, reeling, managed to stand up and follow him to the door.

He turned to face her. "Yeah, I'm gay. Grace has been protecting me, helping me keep my secret. I was going to come out, tell everyone, but I bottled it. I didn't want to let anyone know – not yet. I needed a bit longer." His voice cracked. "I begged her to give me more time; Jason got upset with her but she stuck by me. I saw him in town today and he told me it's over with her. He was pretty angry. I feel terrible, but I'm too much of a coward to call her." He paused and composed himself. "You see, you got Grace so wrong, Kristyn. She comes out better than all of us in this story. She was the one trying to do the right thing and because of the rest of us she's been the most hurt. *I'm* the one making all this mess." He looked at her with a hollow expression on his face, then turned and left.

She stood alone in the hall. All her fantasies about being Prom Queen with Evan her King fell like shattered glass at her feet. She looked at herself in the hall mirror. She stared at her Dior dress, the one Fallon had lent her when she heard about what had happened. She had thought she would be a princess; she had imagined dancing with Evan with this dress swirling around, everyone staring, everyone admiring. She would be his girlfriend, make new friends, be happy at last. Instead she had ruined everything.

What had she been thinking? She'd been a jealous mess. She'd acted like a terrible person. She had never behaved like this before in her life. And now it was the only thing Grace and Evan would think about when they saw her. And she would have to give up the waitressing job too – and she had really enjoyed it. It was her fault: she had done an awful thing – but she hadn't meant to ruin anyone's life. She had just wanted to be at the centre of things for once. It just seemed so many things had gone wrong for her lately that she had lost her sense of reality.

She knew that was no excuse. She had to do something to make things better.

She looked at her watch. It wasn't too late. She texted Grace, "I'm sorry, forget what I asked you to do. Enjoy being Prom Queen."

A text immediately pinged back: "Too late, it's done."

She went up to her room and sat on her bed.

Another ping on her phone. She grabbed it – maybe it wasn't too late. But this one was from Lindsay: "Soz, know I said I'd go with you to prom but have managed to squeeze into Lexie's ride. See you there."

Her mum appeared at her bedroom door. When she had first seen Kristyn all dressed up, her mum had looked so proud of her. Kristyn knew her mum would be devastated if she said she wasn't going now. After all the effort everyone had made to help her get ready.

"Are you ready? Is Lindsay nearly here? The minicab will be arriving in a while."

She was biting back the tears. All that expensive make-up – what a stupid waste! She shook her head. "She's got a lift with someone else, Mum."

She picked up her silver evening bag.

"It's just me."

PART THREE

Prom Night – 7.51 p.m.

CHAPTER 27

Alex

7.51 p.m.

Chris gave Alex the benefit of a brief megawatt smile and then looked down into his glass. "I need a refill – can I get you one?"

She handed over her glass. "Coke, please."

"Now, girl. . ." He leaned in to within inches of her face. "Don't go away, will you."

"Go away?" She was rooted to the spot. All the way here in the limo Chris had kept catching her eye. His meaning couldn't have been clearer. She was his chosen one for the evening. He had just said she looked gorgeous. It was all going to happen. It would be just like a film. It all felt so right. Chris had realized at last that they were made for each other. A boy who would do a red-rose promposal for her: that had to be the right boy, didn't it? She felt a wave of anxiety as she waited for him to come back with the drinks. The actual event was going to happen soon. Their lips would touch. She didn't know whether she felt like screaming or fainting as she saw him working his way back through the crowd. She forced an anxious smile instead.

This was her soulmate.

"Forgot what you said, so I got Fanta – hope that's OK."

She nodded. After all, he hadn't forgotten that she liked roses and that was much more important.

He took a big swig from his glass. "Great prom."

"Yes, yes it is. It's a great theme, Hollywood Nights." *Great*, she groaned inwardly. *And the gold medal for conversation Olympics goes to ... Alex Robertson.*

"Yeah. Good party. Love a good party, me. It's what it's all about, isn't it?"

"Um, yes, I suppose it is. But you like sports too, don't you? The swim team." *Can't I think of anything more interesting to say?*

"Right. Totally. Had a lot of fixtures this term."

Alex was realizing that she had never had an actual conversation with Chris before. They'd always been in a crowd or he was the object of desire on the other side of a classroom. They hadn't been alone together before this moment – if you could call dancing in the midst of hundreds of people being "alone".

It felt like it now.

She wondered if Taylor Lautner was so hard to talk to.

"Which, uh, fixtures are the ones you remember best?" she asked – while to herself she wailed, *It's official. I am the most boring girl in the world.*

How wrong she was: he was off, with a fixture-by-fixture account of the past term's swim meets, no details spared. She tried very hard to concentrate, but when he'd got on to the coach at Hayfield Park disallowing nose clips and something about 4.5-second differences *and* they were still six meets from the end of term, she found her eyes wandering around the room until they alighted on . . . Charlotte.

Charlotte?! What was she doing here?

And she was standing at the doorway talking to Tom. Their heads close together – obviously discussing something intense.

"Alex? Alex?"

She refocused. "Yes, Chris?"

"I think you're really pretty."

Oh God! She felt a wave of panic.

Chris moved his head closer.

"Like, I really like you."

She felt her heart beating at a hundred miles an hour. He *did*, he did really like her – there was no way he would have thought of the red roses if he didn't. Perhaps it was always like this at the beginning; perhaps after the kiss things would be better, more relaxed.

Alex weighed up her options. If she didn't go through with it, she was going to leave tonight exactly the same as when she'd arrived. Never been kissed. It was a thought that after all the build-up to this prom night she simply couldn't bear.

Her eyes flicked up and over to Tom and Charlotte again.

She closed her eyes. So the night didn't feel the way she'd thought it would, the way it looked in the films. Maybe it had been immature of her to expect that. This must be what it was like for everyone – on their first kind of date, conversation was bound to be awkward. Chris was a romantic – he had proven it with the roses – and she was sure the chatting would improve. But it really hadn't been like this in her fantasies. She was surprised it was quite so much of an effort. It never looked this hard in the films, did it? It just sort of flowed in a thrilling kind of a way.

She had obviously expected too much of the evening – so typical of her to get it wrong. She was glad she hadn't told Grace, at least. She bet Grace would laugh if she knew of her ridiculous expectations. And what on earth must Tom have thought when she had been gushing about Chris earlier? She blushed in embarrassment.

She took a deep breath. *I WILL have my first kiss. Come on, Alex, you can do this.*

Just as Chris started to lean in towards her, she heard someone tap the microphone on stage.

CHAPTER 28

Leigh

7.51 p.m.

Right, Leigh thought to herself, *no one is going to help me. I am completely alone in the world.* It had taken her an eternity to walk the mile or so to A&E. She had taken a wrong turn because of the rain, and it had taken her an hour to find her way back to a road she knew. *What had people done before they had GPS on their phones?* Leigh wondered bitterly. She could now see the hospital just up the road, but she felt as though she couldn't take another step. She had taken refuge in a bus shelter, but the seat was broken and she had ended up on the pavement. She was trying to motivate herself to stand up again. *Now I have two choices: I can carry on sitting here feeling sorry for myself like the kind of feeble girl I totally despise, or I can stop whining and do something.* The entrance to A&E was only about a five-minute walk away – but every step was excruciating. She looked in her bag. There was the string she had been tying the stars up with and some gold ribbon. She plaited the ribbon into a fat rope and tied the ends together with the help of her teeth.

She hooked the plaited band over her head and around her neck; then, very carefully, using her good hand, she lifted her wrist and placed it into the makeshift sling. Rolling forward on to her knees, she managed to push herself up into a standing position. Again the world seemed to reel around her for a moment before coming back into focus. She was glad of the cool rain.

OK, Leigh. Walk! She began to put one foot in front of the other. *I shall count steps*, she decided; *that will stop me thinking about anything else. I shall count all the steps until I'm in A&E.*

She was on step two hundred and three when a distant shout intruded into her counting. *That's annoying – where was I?* She had lost count and was just considering whether to take a guess about where she had been or to start again when the voice shouted louder. "Is that voice shouting 'Three! Three!'?" she muttered to herself. "Because that's what it sounds like and it's putting me off. Shut up, voice! And it's a boy's voice. I think I know that boy's voice." She shook her head and tried to focus . . . was she at two hundred and thirty or two hundred and forty?

The shout was nearer now. "Two hundred and thirty-five, that sounds so like Owen, two hundred and thirty-six. . ." She sighed. But he would be on his way to prom with everyone else now, having a lovely time. "Stop it, Leigh!" she growled at herself. *If you'd been a bit more thoughtful about him and Charlotte you might not be in this situation. I did work so hard, though – I can't believe I'm missing it. It's going to be the best prom ever. And I did it all for them.* "Three hundred and twelve, three hundred and thirteen. . ." *Did I? Did I really? Or did I do for me, because if I really had been thinking about them I would have paid them some attention, however busy I was. I truly am the worst kind of girlfriend and friend.* She gave a bark of manic laughter, which made a little girl passing by cling to her mother's legs. *How ironic, in trying to be perfect I end up being the worst. And losing everything I care about. And now I've lost count again. . .*

"Leigh! Leigh! Will you STOP!"

The automatic doors of A&E slid open in front of her but she stopped outside.

She turned round. Owen was there, his face frantic with concern. "God, Leigh, look at you. What happened? Where have you *been*? I got your text and I've been everywhere searching for you – no one had seen you."

Leigh managed a damp smile and threw open her good arm. "Well, here I am! Ta-dah! All ready for my prom."

Owen pulled a face. "What on earth happened? As soon as I got your text I tried to call you back but your phone is off. I went to your house but your mum didn't know where you were – she's frantic, by the way – and then I tried going to the prom venue and when I saw the ladder on the floor and the sequins. . . Here, take my arm. Let's get you inside out of the rain."

After giving her name at reception, asking the nurse to notify her father and phoning her mother, they settled on to the hard seats of the waiting room. Leigh looked at the puddle forming at her feet as the water ran off her dress, and leaned her bedraggled head against the wall behind her. "I know you hate me," she sighed. "I'd hate me. I've been such an idiot. A total idiot. But I wasn't always this stupid, was I? I did use to be a nice person. . ."

Owen gently took her bag, took off his tuxedo jacket and wrapped it round her shoulders.

"So why have I been such an idiot?" She waved her good arm wildly. "Now you DESPISE me. And I totally deserve it. I completely and totally deserve it. I AM A HORRIBLE PERSON!" A few people in the waiting room looked round.

To her surprise, Owen looked as if he was trying not to laugh. "I think you've had a bang on the head and might be a little concussed."

She tentatively felt her head. "Ooh, there is a big bump. Ouch!" She turned to face him with a solemn expression. "I may be a tiny bit woozy – BUT, I'm very clear that I have been a terrible girlfriend and I won't blame you for never, ever, ever, ever. . ."

"Yeah, that's probably enough of the never, evers. . ." Owen grinned.

"I don't blame you for never, ever wanting to see me again." She burst into tears. "Because you are the best boyfriend in the world; you've been so patient and kind when I've been so *not*. I can't imagine not being with you, but you're right, I don't deserve you. . ."

"I never said that," Owen interrupted. "It's just that prom took over your life and I thought you didn't want me – it . . . it . . . felt like that."

"I know," she whispered, taking his hand. "I was really thoughtless and I'm sorry. I didn't deserve you anyway with my perfectionism and my bossy ways. Well, I've certainly learned my lesson. Look at me. All the bossiness in the world, all that planning for perfection, and this is where I am on prom night." She noticed the waiting-room clock and jumped. "Hey! You must get going, Owen. It's started. You can't miss the big surprise."

He took her face in his hands and stared into her eyes. "I'm not going anywhere. I know that you wanted it to be a special night; I know you like things to be perfect and can go a little crazy trying to do it. You have been on Planet Prom – but you know what? It is going to be the best prom ever – and you know why?"

She shook her head.

"Because we are going be together – possibly rather late, but the important thing is that we'll be *together*."

She looked into his eyes, "Really? *Together together*? You can forgive Promzilla?"

"I can forgive Promzilla. And now I'm going to kiss you – very, very gently because I don't want to hurt your arm, but I have to kiss you right this minute. Is that OK?"

She nodded her head, and as she felt his lips on hers she felt that not even the best prom in the world could beat the feeling of happiness and relief that flooded through her.

"Ahem."

They broke away from their embrace to find a tall figure in surgical scrubs staring down at them.

"Someone told me my daughter was in need of medical assistance."

CHAPTER 29

Charlotte

7.51 p.m.

Well, she had been stood up, she thought morosely as she walked towards the exit, trying to hold back her tears.

And she had spent ages getting ready at home, in front of the mirror.

Charlotte's fingers had refused to obey her brain and had smudged red lipstick way outside the lines. *Maybe he likes clowns*, she had thought, snatching another tissue and rubbing make-up remover into her face for what seemed like the hundredth time. What had made it extra annoying was that she had done two make-up sessions already that day, and although she hadn't quite finished Leigh's because of their row, her hand had been as steady as a surgeon's for the other girls. *So why* can't *I do my own?*

She had thrown the lipstick down on the dressing table and flopped on to her bed. The kitten hopped on to her chest. *Why am I going to some random venue?* she agonized. *I mean, I've only met him for five minutes. I don't know him. It's crazy. I hate feeling like this. I'm not going.*

But she knew she was. She hadn't been able to stop thinking about the record-shop boy all day and the thought of seeing him again had made her stomach turn somersaults. "God," she'd wailed to the ceiling, "if this is what liking a boy is like it should come with a health warning. What if it meant nothing to him and I turn up and he's embarrassed that I took him seriously?" She'd picked up the kitten and lifted it up in front of her face. "Aaargh . . . I don't know what to doooo. . ."

"*Please?*" She could hear his voice asking her. He

had sounded genuine. He really had. But what did she know?

She'd brought the purring kitten's face close to hers. "Look, Kitten, if I don't go, I'll never know. If it's a disaster, you say I'm brave enough and tough enough to deal with it, whatever happens. It's not as though I've got anything else on tonight. Everyone's at prom. No one was interested in my anti-prom party except you. They all appeared to want to dress up and go to that mad showing-off and popularity contest."

Putting the purring kitten down, she had got up and took out her lipstick again, "So, if I don't go out tonight I'll never know what might have happened. If I *do* go. . ." – she had stared at her lipstick as if they were about to do battle – "at least I won't spend the rest of my life wondering. I know what my dad would have said."

She had given the lipstick a hard glare. "OK, lipstick, it's you and me and we are going to take a chance. This roller coaster has started and we're not getting off till the end of the ride."

*

The thing that didn't make any sense, she thought to herself, reaching the exit, was how she had ended up at prom. She could understand being stood up – she should have known better than to put any faith in something a boy said – but to have ended up at the one place she never would have voluntarily gone to. . . She wondered darkly if Leigh had had something to do with this.

"Charlotte!" Zoe called to her, as she was about to open the door to leave. "I'm so pleased you're here! You haven't heard from Leigh, have you?"

Charlotte frowned. "Leigh still hasn't arrived? That's strange. I mean, that's more than strange. I saw her earlier, at the Style House – but that was ages ago."

"Was she all right?" Zoe asked.

Charlotte didn't know what to say. "She was certainly talking about nothing but prom."

"So she didn't give a reason why she wouldn't turn up?"

"No! The opposite."

Zoe frowned. "I can't imagine what would keep her from her own prom."

Charlotte felt a sense of alarm. If something had stopped Leigh from being here, it must be big.

Zoe disappeared to look outside.

Her own prom – Charlotte thought about Zoe's words. This was prom. All around her. She wandered into the main room, taking in the LA skyline, the chocolate fountain, the candyfloss booth, the Hollywood cocktail bar, even those wretched pink marshmallows which were the perfect powder-pink Leigh had wanted. This was definitely Leigh's prom. Charlotte had heard about every detail, apart from, obviously, the most important detail of all – the venue. Charlotte turned her head up towards the gold glittery stars spinning slowly in the lights above her. She stopped short. Was she seeing things? One had her photo on it.

Why would Leigh do that?

She began to search the crowd and with a growing sense of unease realized that Leigh was still nowhere to be seen. Only everyone else from her year. At their prom. When she got back to where she'd started, she gazed up again. She recognized the photo – it had been taken at Leigh's last birthday party; she knew that green dress. Leigh had cut herself out of the photo so it was just Charlotte's face, but she could just make out Leigh's hand on her shoulder and they had been laughing at . . . what? She couldn't recall exactly; she just remembered they hadn't been able to stop and had collapsed on the lawn in giggles. They hadn't laughed like that for a long time. She missed that.

She took a deep breath. Had Leigh somehow worked with her mystery boy to get her here?

But there was no Leigh and no mystery boy.

Disappointment, anxiety and anger hit her all at once.

What was going on?

CHAPTER 30

Grace

7.51 p.m.

"I don't deserve this," Kristyn said wretchedly from the stage. "I'm not the one who should be wearing it." She suddenly burst into tears and tore the crown from her head. The whole school gawped in confusion as she ran from the stage.

"Well, that has to be the shortest Prom Queen reign *ever*," Alex whispered. She raised her eyebrows at Grace and went on, "What happened there? I mean, *seriously?*"

Grace could guess, but she didn't say anything. A bewildered Mrs Keane leapt in and swiftly introduced Evan. *He* wouldn't let her down with his speech. Grace could see Mrs Keane beaming at him: Evan was going to be a perfect Prom King. No surprises with *him*. Mrs Keane handed him the microphone and stepped back.

He caught Grace's eye in the crowd and managed a smile. She smiled back. In spite of everything she was happy that he was going to have this moment. Even though she had lost her relationship with Jason for it, she'd get over the pain of that, one day – and wasn't it more important that she had stood by her friend?

Alex whispered to her, "Don't want to stress you out, Grace, but your mum and dad are here. Did they come for the Prom Queen announcement? I can see them at the back – your mum seems to be being revived. Ooh, dearie, she does *not* look a happy bunny."

Grace didn't even turn round. Evan had started talking.

"Hi, everyone."

Grace could hear the tremor in his voice and saw that his knuckles were white on the microphone.

"I want to say thanks for voting for me. It means a lot, more than I can say. Here we all are, together for the last time. I can't believe that we're all leaving Harper High. It seems like we only started yesterday. Over the past five years you've been everything friends should be. You've stuck with me through thick and thin. You're all so smart and funny and honest. Yes, honest – especially you, Tom, who told me my new yellow shirt sucked and turned my boy-band dreams to dust by pointing out the tiny detail that singing talent was a requirement. I still beg to differ." Evan paused as the audience laughed. "I don't know how the years have gone by so fast but now we're all leaving. We're all grown-up and going on to the rest of our lives. I hope they're all everything you want them to be. I'll always remember the friends I made here, and tonight I especially want to say thank you to someone who has been a very special friend to me."

All eyes turned to Grace.

"Yes, Grace – she has been the best friend in the world. She has always been there for me. But I have to ask myself: have I been a good friend to her? No, not really, not at all."

People were beginning exchange puzzled glances.

He looked around the crowd of faces in front of him. "And I've not been such a great friend to all of you, either. Because friends are honest with each other and I haven't been honest with you. I've kept something from you."

No one moved a muscle.

"I want to say sorry for that. I'm sorry I didn't trust you. Sorry that I was afraid of being mocked, afraid of aggression, afraid of losing friends. But Grace made me realize that I have to trust the people I care about. And be true to myself. Kristyn has just done me a big favour. You don't know it, but she's just showed that the truth isn't always the easy way; it can be messy – it can hurt and take courage." He took a deep breath.

The room was completely silent.

Evan went on. "I certainly didn't plan on doing this in front of the whole school. But what the hell – if Kristyn can find the courage to tell you all the truth, so can I. Grace, because of my secret you've lost the person you really love" – he found her face again – "so I'm going to do what you've been saying I should have done a long time ago." He paused and took a deep breath. "I'm gay. There you have it. It's part of who I am, what makes me . . . me. I hope that all of you who have been my friends over the past five years will still be my friends now, because this is who I really am. This is me." He fell silent.

The room appeared to be holding its breath. Evan stood there alone in the spotlight, suddenly a stark, lonely figure.

"That's it. That's all I have to say."

There was a pause, a beat – before the air rocked with the roar of cheering as the room erupted.

Mrs Keane and Miss Summerfield were staring at each other in stunned silence before Grace saw Mrs Keane mouth "What the hell!" at Miss Summerfield and they both joined in the yelling and clapping as hard as they could.

"Oops!" Alex laughed. "Don't look now, Grace, but I think your mum is actually having a heart attack. I can't believe it – how could you have kept this a secret from me?"

Grace looked at Evan.

"Well, OK, I guess it wasn't your secret to tell . . ." Alex continued, "but . . . who is the secret boy – or *person*, should I say, as we've all suddenly gone very modern and I don't want to presume. . ."

Grace smiled. "Boy," she said, before being overwhelmed by a now familiar ache, "and I don't know where he is."

"He's here," said a deep voice behind her – and two warm arms encircled her.

"Jason!" Her heart flipped and she spun round, the cream and gold lace of her dress swirling around her ankles. "Jason! Jason! Jason!" She flung herself into his arms.

Over his shoulder she saw Evan had found his way through the congratulating crowd to her side.

Jason extracted himself from her and solemnly shook Evan's hand. "Good job, mate. That took bravery. Well done."

Evan shook his head, "Should have done it a long time ago. I wanted to apologize and say thank you for . . . you know, everything. I'm sorry. Start again?"

Jason smiled and pulled Evan into a bear hug. "New start."

Tom and Ben came up, and Evan stood looking at them; Grace could tell he was tense.

"Come here, you idiot," Tom grinned, grabbing Evan in another big hug. "Should have guessed it when you bought that freaking awful shirt."

Ben stood awkwardly until Tom released Evan, then held out his hand. "Good call, mate." Evan reached out his hand to take it. "Aww, what the hell!" Ben guffawed and enveloped Evan in his huge frame.

Grace was enjoying watching the relief on Evan's face when Tony from their English class appeared. He gave Evan a level stare.

Evan frowned. "You OK, Tony?"

Tony nodded and looked Evan right in the eye. "Want to dance?"

Grace caught Evan's look of confusion – then understanding. A huge smile broke and lit up his whole face. "Really?" he asked, as if he could hardly believe it.

"Sure, why not? I guess it's goodbye-to-secrets night and I don't see why you should get all the attention. God knows I've waited long enough for you." Tony gestured towards the dance floor. "Don't tell me you're chicken after that performance."

Distracted by Tony and Evan, Grace and Jason became aware of the disturbance coming towards them only at the last minute.

"I'd better make myself disappear," Jason whispered and took his hand out of hers.

Grace snatched it back. "Don't you dare go anywhere! Time to make some introductions, Jason."

"Grace! Grace!" Her mother appeared, snapping through the crowd like a dragon out of a volcano, her father in tow.

"Oh God, she did wear her prom dress," Grace sighed, as a vision in yards of yellow net appeared in front of her, obviously struggling to control itself.

Breathing heavily, her mother glared at Evan. "You," she exclaimed, jabbing at his tuxedo with a red talon, "you are a liar and a disgrace and . . . and . . . you will *never* see my daughter again. What a terrible shock for your poor parents, and your father so high in his profession. To think I let you out alone with Grace . . . that I *trusted* you. . ."

"Well, look on the bright side," Evan grinned, "she couldn't have been in safer hands."

Jason, Grace and Tony tried to stifle their giggles.

"Come on, Tony, let's dance." Evan and Tony headed off.

Her mother whipped round. "You again," she sneered icily at Jason, "and who may I ask, are *you*?"

Something snapped in Grace. "How *dare* you speak to Jason like that? How dare you? To someone you've never even spoken to? He's my boyfriend, Mum; we've been going out for six months and he's the most—" Grace felt Jason put a calming hand on her arm.

"I'm Jason Roberts. I work as an apprentice chef at The Bay Tree. Pleased to meet you." He held out his hand.

Grace's mother stared at it as if it were on fire. "A chef? A *chef*? Doug, Doug. . ." She pushed Grace's father forward. "Grace, your father and I want you to come home this minute. We shall sort out the Prom Queen fiasco on Monday in an appointment with Mrs Keane. And if you think you are *ever* going out of the house between now and Oxford you have another think coming. And . . . Doug. . ." She gestured towards Jason. "Tell this boy to leave, please, and that he won't be seeing our daughter again. As if she would be seen with a . . . a . . . kitchen person."

"No."

Her mother did a double take as her father suddenly pulled himself up to his full height.

"No, I won't. I think that Jason appears to be a very polite young man and that he must be extremely talented to have a job at The Bay Tree. It's an excellent restaurant. Jason, I have every faith that Grace makes good choices in her friends. Allow me to shake your hand."

Her mother opened and closed her mouth – but before she could say anything her father went on, "And if Evan wasn't having such a lively time on the dance floor I'd shake his hand, too. That can't have been easy and I can understand all too well the reasons that both he *and* Grace had for their actions. But now, no more lies. For any of us. Understood?"

Grace flung her arms round her father's neck and hugged him tight. "Understood totally. Thanks, Dad," she whispered.

"How dare you!" Her mother was gasping as if drowning. "Don't you care about what's best for Grace? I'm telling you now, Jason and Evan are not welcome at the after-prom party. No one is after

Grace's deception. It's cancelled."

"No, it's not," her father said firmly. "It's my house too, my money paid for it and I shall have who I please to the party. Jason and Evan are most welcome. As are all Grace's friends. It's about time she had her own life. Her own dreams. She's not a little girl any more. Seems she has found her voice today. Time to let her fly now."

"Doug!" her mother screeched. "What's the matter with you?"

"I think I might have found my voice too, my dear. A little late – but what do they say? Better late than never. Now turn around, my little lemon sherbet, and head for the doorway. We've got a lot of people turning up for a party very soon."

Grace watched in astonishment as her mother, mouth still opening and closing like a goldfish, meekly turned and headed towards the exit. Her dad turned back to wink at her before disappearing after her.

Grace put her arms round Jason. "I'm sorry," she said, "for not being considerate enough of your feelings. . ."

He pulled her close. "No, *I*'m sorry. I didn't trust

you enough; I thought you'd never be able to stand up to your mum. But I was wrong! You were amazing. Time for one last dance?"

She melted into his arms.

He whispered into her ear, "I would kiss you, but. . ."

"But what?"

"I only kiss *official* Prom Queens."

"Shut up!" she giggled.

"So what happened?"

"It's a very long story."

"Tell me."

But before she could open her mouth, Jason's lips were on hers and her heart was singing like a freed bird.

CHAPTER 31

Kristyn

7.51 p.m.

Kristyn fled. She found herself outside in the car park. It felt like the end of everything.

She sat on the wall of the car park, rocking back and forth with shame and misery.

She knew it was the end. The end of any hope that she could ever see anyone from school again.

She had seen the way Lindsay whispered to Lexie, laughing at her as she ran off the stage.

And the people she now respected – Evan, Grace,

Jason. They must all hate her. She was sure they would have told everyone else by now. She couldn't blame them. She had done a horrible, mean thing.

She would have given anything to turn the clock back. She would even go back to being the mouse, grateful for a crumb of attention from someone like Lindsay's table. A mouse. She knew that was what Lindsay must call her.

She would have to take that salon job now. There was no way she was going to sixth-form college. She couldn't see anyone from school again, not every day, all looking at her and knowing what she'd done – it would be torture. The Style House wasn't what she wanted – but what else was there now? At least her mum and dad would be pleased she'd stop going on about staying at college and doing fashion. Jessie was always telling her it was a stupid idea anyway. Kristyn sighed. But that's what she was – stupid. Time to stop dreaming and realize what she was: a dull, talentless, stupid, mean. . ."

"Hey, Kristyn," a voice said gently.

She started and looked up. "Jessie? What are you doing here?"

"I came to find you. They said you might be out here. I have something to tell you. Something important. It's about the Style House."

Kristyn tried to smile. *Stop being selfish and be grateful*, she said to herself. "If the junior job has come up at last, of course I'll take it. Thank you, Jessie."

Her sister sighed and took her hand. "Look, Kristyn, I know you don't want that job."

"I do, really I do," Kristyn protested weakly.

"No you don't, you liar, liar, pants on fire. You never have. I've pushed Mum and Dad and you about that job because . . . because. . ."

"Because what?"

"Because I thought the fact you obviously didn't want to work there was like saying it wasn't good enough for you. As though what I did wasn't good enough – you know, working in a hairdresser's."

"But you love it – you're the top stylist in the whole town!"

"I know. And I do love it, with all my heart – and that's because I love my work. And I'm good at it. Guess I always wanted to be to the big, successful, favourite daughter – but I always knew you were smarter than me. And you really have a talent for fashion. I saw that when you couldn't keep your mouth shut while Fallon's stylist was in the salon today. She listened to you. And Fallon went with all your suggestions."

Kristyn thought back to sorting through the racks, pulling out outfits, accessorizing them – it had been the best fun ever. And then Fallon had asked how she could thank her, and Li had jumped in and told the story of the dress and then. . . She looked down at her beautiful dress. Well, it didn't matter any more, did it?

"I saw a different you then, Kristyn. You were confident. You were doing what *you* loved. I realized then that you've *got* to go to college. I went home and spoke to Mum and Dad; it took a long time but they listened to me and they've agreed." Jessie beamed at her. "So what about that, hey? You're going to college, going to be a fashionista and leave your big sister way behind. Promise me you'll still style me when you're famous?"

Kristyn shook her head.

"What? What are you shaking your head for? I thought you'd be dancing!"

"I can't go. I don't *want* to go. To college."

Jessie eyes were round with disbelief. "Are you kidding me? It's all you've ever talked about."

"I've changed my mind."

Jessie took a deep breath. "OK. So you're saying you *don't* want to do fashion at college. You don't want to work for someone like Fallon Fernandez, despite the fact that she said you had real talent and would be interested in hiring you once you graduate. You *want* to work as a junior in my salon, the job you clearly have hated the idea of since it was first mentioned."

Kristyn nodded her head dumbly.

Jessie was exasperated. "I don't know what to say. There is no job at the moment, so your new dream of working in the salon will have to wait." She scrutinized her sister closely. "I don't know what's going on with you. We can talk about this later. Maybe your friends can talk some sense into you." She walked off with her hands in her pockets.

Kristyn was close to tears. Her dream of college, right within her grasp . . . but she couldn't. Not now. It was impossible. Suddenly seeing Grace and Jason making a beeline for her, she gasped in horror – then hung her head low, wishing she was a chameleon.

"Hi, Kristyn," Grace said, sitting next to her on the wall.

Kristyn was aching with holding back tears. "I'm so sorry, Grace. I don't know what else to say. I behaved so badly. I deserve all the hate I'm going to get. I know I do. I was just . . . jealous. And that's no excuse. You didn't deserve it."

"No, I didn't," Grace responded calmly. "But I do owe you a thank you."

"What?" Kristyn thought she must have misheard.

"I owe you a thank you. You didn't have to say anything up there on stage, but you did. And everyone saw what it cost you to do it. Because you were honest and did the right thing in the end, Evan felt he could come out. . ."

Kristyn stared in shock.

"Yup," Grace nodded, "he did. In front of the whole school. And he wouldn't have if you hadn't led the way with the baring-the-soul stuff. You ended up doing me a favour. With one bound I was free!" Grace threw her hands in the air and laughed. She grabbed

Jason's hand. "And now the whole world can know about me and Jason."

Kristyn managed a smile. "I'm really and truly glad for you. I tried to call you earlier, Jason, to tell you to come, to get you back with Grace, but. . ."

"I saw on my phone, but I was already on my way. But thanks, anyway, for trying. . ."

Grace stood up. "Look, I know you're sorry. Anyone can see how bad you're feeling. Come back in with us. No one really knows anything – except Evan, and he sort of owes you too. Could we start again?"

Kristyn thought she must be dreaming. "Yes," she answered with all her heart. "Please."

"Come on, then – we don't want to miss the big surprise everyone's talking about."

As they entered the heat and noise of the main room, Lindsay suddenly appeared, her face contorted with anger. She grabbed Kristyn's arm and roughly pulled her aside.

"Hey!" Grace protested.

Lindsay's face was in Kristyn's. "What do you mean by telling Jed I cheated in the test today?"

Kristyn was confused. "I don't know what. . ."

"Don't pretend you don't know. It must have been you. Turns out Jed worked his guts out for that test and isn't '*impressed by girls who cheat*'. I thought you were my friend, you cow, you dropped me right in the dirt and after all I've done for you. . ."

Grace stepped between them. "If I may," she said calmly. "Two points of error, Lindsay: one, Kristyn is *not* your friend any more; two, the reason is that you haven't done anything except use her—"

"Oh, is that right?" Lindsay snapped. "Well answer me this, then: who else knew I had her paper, apart from Lexie, who is a *real* friend? Who else but her?"

"That would be me." Grace smiled. "Perhaps you shouldn't go shooting your mouth off about what you did on the phone quite so loudly. You do have a *very* er . . . foghorn voice."

Grace and Jason took Kristyn firmly by each arm and led her off to the dance floor.

"You look incredible in that dress, by the way," Grace said. "Dior?"

She nodded. "I had a lucky break today."

Grace raised her eyebrows. "I'll say! It's amazing. You really know how to put an outfit together. We should go shopping together sometime. I have such a hard time finding things that work for me. Maybe you could help?"

"Sure." Kristyn now knew she must be dreaming. She was dancing with Grace, Jason, Tom, Charlotte, Alex, Ben, Zoe, Evan and Tony, all the people she liked the most at school. And they didn't hate her.

A boy from her history class was dancing closer and closer to her. "Coming to Grace's after-prom party?" he said hopefully.

"Yes, she is!" Grace yelled, winking at her.

"Our last night at Harper High!" Alex yelled. "Roll on sixth-form college."

Kristyn smiled. When this dance was over she needed to send a message to her sister.

The End of the Night

CHAPTER 32

Leigh

8.30 p.m.

"A crutch, Dad? Must I?"

"Yes – you've sprained your ankle and fractured your wrist." He tapped the hard cast, which Leigh had chosen in blue to match her dress. "You're lucky I'm letting you go to prom at all, even if it is just for the end. All the excitement will be over by now. . ."

"Nothing about prom seems so important now," Leigh sighed, leaning into Owen's shoulder. "Everyone can manage without me. I'm sure it will be fine!" She stopped and laughed out loud. "'Fine'! Listen to me!"

Her Dad looked at Owen. "Shall I call a cab, then?"

Owen smiled. "No need, Dr Kowalski – I've arranged something."

As she hobbled towards the exit past the cubicles she glanced at her reflection. A nurse had lent her some thread and her dress was slightly less ragged, and at least the main slash had been sewn up. She had dried out and redone her make-up. It wasn't as good as Charlotte's, but it didn't matter any more. It would do! She laughed again. Had she really said that? And her hair, all that expensive salon styling, washed out. She had hung her head upside down under the hand-dryer in the toilets and brushed it through.

"I'm sorry I'm not quite the gorgeous creature I should have been tonight," she sighed to Owen.

"Are you kidding? You look amazing. I love your hair long like that, all shiny and natural. You look like a princess." The automatic doors swung open on to a landscape washed cleaned by the rain. The building was now bathed in the pink and gold of early sunset. Leigh stood rooted to the spot in astonishment.

"And you know what happens to princesses. . ." Owen smiled. Outside A&E was a delicate white carriage drawn by two grey horses, who were swishing their long manes and jingling the silver bells on their blue harnesses. The coachman, in blue uniform, jumped down and opened the carriage door.

"Time for your prom, Leigh," Owen grinned, holding out his hand to help her inside. "You shall go to the ball."

Leigh gave a squeak of joy. She was the luckiest girl in the world. Not because she was going to prom, but because she had someone who cared about her, even after the way she had acted.

When they arrived, the best thing about it was not that it looked like a perfect Hollywood night, nor that everyone was congratulating her on pulling off the best prom ever, but the welcome she got from her friends. People fell on her with cries of genuine concern and delighted welcome when they realized that she was all right. This was what it was all about. Caring about people and friends.

"I forgot," she said.

"Forgot what?" Owen asked.

"All my lists, all those timetables. I forgot to put in the most important things."

"What were they?"

"Friends. Family. You."

He squeezed her hand and kissed her.

Everything was going to be all right.

"Leigh! Leigh! Oh my god! What happened to you? Are you OK? We've all been worried sick!" The normally cool Charlotte was almost hysterical with anxiety.

"Don't panic – I'm fine. Fell off a ladder. How come *you're* here? What changed your mind? I'm so, so happy to see you. Even if it was putting up your star that made me fall."

"Oh no. That's terrible. But why? Why did you even *make* one for me?"

"Because I just wanted you to be here, even if it was only a photo."

"And that's all?"

Leigh looked puzzled. "Yes. Why?"

"You didn't, you know, *do* anything to get me to come here?"

"*Do?* No. What on earth are you on about?"

Charlotte seemed to slump a little. "No, nothing."
Then she leaned in again. "Are you *sure*?"

"The only thing I did to get you here is wish it with
all my heart. And it came true. I'm sorry, Charlotte –
I've been an idiot and a rubbish friend. I know you
didn't want to have anything to do with prom and I
should have respected that." She pulled a face. "Can
you forgive me?"

Charlotte gave Leigh a gentle hug and whispered,
"I might have got slightly more involved in prom than
you think. . ."

Leigh looked puzzled. "What are you talking
about?"

Charlotte pointed at Ben. Ben! With a new haircut
which had tamed his long dark curls into a slick, smart
style, a fitted white dress shirt, bow tie and well-made
tuxedo, it was hard to recognize him.

"Wow! What happened to him? Talk about a
makeover."

Tom had appeared. "All my own work. But that's
not the biggest surprise. What's the time? Nearly the
moment."

Leigh stared into the crowd. "Moment for what?" Then she clutched Charlotte's arm. "Oh my god – is that *Zoe*? And why are Lindsay and Lexie giggling behind her?"

"Watch and wait, Leigh. Watch and wait."

Zoe looked like a movie star in a vintage film. Her hair was styled in a short wave, shiny and cute. Her full lips were a dark red which looked amazing against her pale, smooth complexion, and her green eyes shone, lined like a cat's with Charlotte's trademark perfect eyeliner. Zoe opened her sequinned bag, which matched the vintage evening dress Charlotte had lent her that afternoon, took out a card and opened it nervously. Lindsay, behind her, collapsed laughing.

Zoe looked at her watch, held her head up and began to walk steadily towards the edge of the dance floor, where Chris and Alex were dancing.

Lindsay nudged Lexie and mouthed, "She's actually going to do it!" But her face fell as Zoe walked straight past Chris without appearing even to notice him and stood in front of Ben – who was standing there, staring at her with his mouth open.

He looked as if he was about to pass out, but whatever Zoe said to him must have been magic, because with a stunned expression he took her hand and led her on to the dance floor.

"So what did it say on the card?" Leigh asked.

"*Originally*, it said, 'This is your promposal. I want the last dance with you and only you. Whatever I'm doing, whoever I'm with, please come up to me and claim this dance. Chris.'"

"'Chris'?" Leigh gasped. "I don't understand."

"And neither do Lindsay and Lexie. They sent a fake promposal to Zoe from Chris. But I heard what they had planned, went past Zoe's house where it was plonked on the doorstep with a bunch of rubbish garage flowers and I, er . . . swapped the cards – same message, different boy."

"Imagine if she had gone up to Chris!" Leigh frowned.

"I know. She would have died. I think that was the point, wasn't it? Let's face it, he's not Mr Sensitive, is he?" Tom said darkly.

Zoe and Ben looked as if they had started a conversation that wasn't going to finish for a long time. Leigh gave Charlotte a squeeze. "You're a big softie, really, aren't you? But I still don't know what changed your mind about coming. I know, I know, you tried to tell me and I wasn't listening. I know it's all a bit crazy and nothing worked out according to plan, but having you here and having Owen here, all my friends – that's the important thing, isn't it?"

Charlotte gave her another hug. "It is, Leigh. It is. And actually it hasn't been total torture seeing everyone here."

"I *told* you."

"But I'm going now."

"But there's still half an hour left."

'I'm sorry, but I'm not really in the mood."

Leigh sighed. "But you'll miss the big surprise."

CHAPTER 33

Charlotte

8.45 p.m.

As she wandered towards the exit, she was pleased for Leigh that everything had gone so well after all her hard work. But Charlotte's evening was over; her friends had got her to stay much longer than she had meant to. To be honest, they had really helped her take her mind off things, and she had still hoped . . . but not any more.

She had read the mystery boy completely wrong, made a huge mistake, the same way she had thought she could write songs. What a joke! Well, now she knew that he hadn't really been interested. She had totally imagined the connection between them. What a fool she had been. And her songwriting . . . she was obviously no good, so that had been a fantasy too. She felt bad about saying no to the after-prom party, but she had never been going to go. She wanted to be on her own now.

"LADIES AND GENTLEMEN!" The music cut out and a voice boomed out from the microphone. On the stage a drum kit had appeared, along with some mikes.

Charlotte turned to see Leigh being helped up on to the stage to stand next to the owner of the booming voice. She recognized him immediately: the massive tall figure of Rob Harrison, head of Starlight Records, the biggest record company in America. What was *he* doing here?

"First of all, I want to say welcome to tonight's surprise event." He got out an envelope. "We're going to announce the winner of the British element of the Starlight singer–songwriter competition right here, right now, and one of the newest and biggest bands in the States are going to sing it as part of their set tonight. We went live on MTV five minutes ago."

The Triangle erupted in cheers, but Charlotte's heart sank. Not only had she been duped into coming to prom and stood up by the only guy she had ever really been interested in, but now they were going to announce the winner of the competition she had entered, the competition she would have done anything to win.

"First let me introduce the band and their first number, which will be the winning song: can you all give a big hand for . . . the Human Animals!"

Charlotte immediately recognized the dark-haired boy who had pulled her mystery boy out of the record shop. She felt excitement and terror at the same time as she saw her mystery boy, bounding on to the stage behind him and grabbing the microphone.

He started to sing:

"The way you move is in my head,
I hear your voice,
I know your smile."

She could hardly breathe. That was *her* song? And her mystery boy was Jackson Rivers – lead singer of the Human Animals? What was going on?

As he twisted the mike, crying out her words as if he might break, she saw immediately that he was straining to spot someone in the crowd. It couldn't be her, could it? She looked away. She wasn't going to make that mistake again.

Why hadn't she known anything about this?

She felt her phone vibrate. *God, not now. Who?*

It was her mum, shrieking down the phone at her. "You've won, you've won! You never told me! How dare you! I've just found the envelope under the kitten's blanket. I think it's been there a few days by the state of it. Oh my god! Is that your song playing now? Who's playing it? No, don't tell me. Enjoy yourself and tell me later. Have a great, *great* evening. You deserve it. Bye. . ."

"Stop, Mum – wait, before you go. . ."

Behind her the music had stopped and Jackson was saying, "And that song was written by Charlotte Lau – who remains a mystery girl, so if you're watching, Charlotte, you need to contact Starlight Records. . ."

Her mother shrieked again.

"Mum. Listen. Do you fancy an all-expenses-paid trip to New York? It's the prize along with the recording contract."

Her mum's scream went off the Richter scale.

Well, at least she had been wrong that she was a rubbish songwriter. A little flame of hope ignited in her chest as she wondered if she had been wrong about anything else.

Leigh had managed to climb down from the stage and was all over her, as was everyone around her.

"Why didn't you say?" Leigh yelled. "You crazy girl. Why didn't you *say*?"

Charlotte laughed. "I didn't *know*! I tried to tell you I had entered but you were always too busy. And why didn't *you* tell *me* this was going to happen?"

"Wasn't allowed. Big record-company secret. Now shut up, Miss Songwriter! Just enjoy your fame and watch the show."

When the band eventually crashed out the final chord of their set, the boy jumped down from the front of the stage like an acrobat. In front of hundreds of pairs of eyes he worked his way through people trying to talk to him – until he was standing straight in front of her. "Hello, Beret Girl. Sorry I'm late. There was a problem with the sound system so we went on late. Did you like the song?"

"It's mine."

He looked at her in amazement. "No kidding?"

"No kidding."

"You're a freaking genius, then!" he cried, grabbing her hands and twirling her round. "And the best part is . . . apart from finding you here, I thought I'd die thinking you might imagine I'd bailed on our date."

"Date?"

Mrs Keane had given permission for the DJ to play another song.

"Come and dance?"

She let him lead her on to the dance floor and put his arms round her. Nothing had ever felt so right before.

"Can I see you again?"

She looked up into his green eyes. "You live in California."

"Ah, but guess where we record?" Her heart jumped as he rested his cheek against hers and whispered into her ear, "New York." She couldn't speak, and he drew his face back from hers. "Hey, I don't want to come on too strong, I know we only just met, but for me, well it wasn't like just meeting any girl. I meet loads of girls but I have never, never wanted to talk to a girl like I wanted to talk to you."

"It's true." The dark-haired boy who was dancing nearby with a swooning girl grinned. "He's been impossible ever since he met you. If you hadn't still been here I think it would have broken the band up."

"I'd like to see you in New York, Jackson River," she murmured.

"Hey, you know my name, Beret Girl – or should I say Charlotte Lau?"

"Of course I do. I knew everything about you. Except what you looked like."

He looked round the room at the dancers as people began to clear up around them. "Don't you love prom? This one looks as if it's been fantastic. Everyone so happy. Best one I've ever been to by a mile," he said gently, kissing her softly on the mouth and pulling her close to his chest.

After what seemed like a long time, she pulled away and looked around her. She was surrounded by all her friends – all looking the happiest she'd ever seen them. "Maybe prom's not so bad after all," she smiled, before feeling his lips on hers again.

CHAPTER 34

Alex

8.59 p.m.

The DJ was playing a slow number. Chris held out his hand. "So how about that dance you promised me?" He winked at her.

She put her glass down and allowed him to pull her into his arms.

"Nice dress," he said.

"Thanks." She was trying to concentrate on not treading on his toes. "The band was amazing," she sighed, staring into Chris's face. "I mean, it *was*, wasn't it – don't you think?"

"Yeah. I mean who doesn't like the Human Animals? Pretty awesome having them here on prom night."

"And Charlotte winning the competition – that was just incredible, wasn't it?"

"Yeah, but it did interrupt—"

"And Evan, too – that was so brave." Alex knew she should shut up but her mouth appeared to be determined to keep going.

Chris shrugged. "Weird. He's probably fancied me all this time. Hope he doesn't make a move. . ." He looked at her. "And talking of making a move. . ." He leaned in.

Alex knew no surprise Starlight Records announcement was going to stop her first kiss now. She closed her eyes again and tried to get her mouth into what she thought would be a good position – but instead, her mouth said, "I just wanted to say thank you for the roses." *What* was *the matter with her, for goodness' sake?*

Chris drew back. "What?"

"The roses. You know. I said I liked them in the art room."

"Huh?"

Alex pulled back a step. "Um, yeah, and that promposal you sent me . . . red roses saying 'PROM' with a question mark."

Chris threw back his head and guffawed. "Seriously? How lame is that? Sure it wasn't Evan? Sounds more like something his kind would do."

Alex's wrenched herself out of Chris's grasp as she realized what he had said. "What do you mean? Do you mean 'care enough about someone to think about what *they* might like'? Oh my god – Tom was right: you are a complete and total jerk."

"Hey!" Chris grabbed her arm. "I thought this is what you wanted. I'll buy you a bunch of stupid daffodils if that's what you want – now, come on. . ." He tried to catch hold of her arm.

She was too quick for him. "*Roses*, you idiot!" she cried.

Suddenly she felt two warm arms around her and a voice in her ear saying, "Red roses, weren't they? That's what I heard were your favourites."

She looked up into Tom's deep brown eyes. "*You!*" she gasped.

"Hey!" Chris yelled again. "What are you doing? She's with me."

"Not any more," Tom answered and pulled her closer.

Chris glared at him – but Tom was taller and fitter than him by a long way and he backed off.

"*And* I asked for a Coke," she called after him.

"Coke?" Tom asked, as she rested her head on his chest.

"Doesn't matter," she smiled, before daring to ask, "So why did you do it?"

"Why do you think, Sherlock?"

She buried her head in his shoulder. "I don't want to say. I've got everything so totally wrong. I am the dimmest girl in Dim Town. I'm scared of getting it wrong again."

"You won't get it wrong."

"OK. So how long have I been too stupid to know about this?"

Tom scratched his head. "Oh not long, like about FOR EVER. I was beginning to think we'd never get here. I really thought the roses would work."

"But it didn't put you off – seeing me in my Paddington onesie and with oil dripping down my nose?"

"But it's such a *pretty* nose," he said, kissing the tip of it.

Alex felt she was truly dreaming – dreaming the most astonishing dream of her life. "I thought . . . I thought maybe you liked Charlotte." She looked over at Charlotte, deep in the arms of Jackson.

"What? Not like that. She wanted me to help her out with Ben and Zoe. Which appears to have been a good plan, as it looks as if they've both found their soulmate at last."

"Why didn't you just *tell* me that the flowers were from you?"

"What? To add to the humiliation? Not only did it not occur to you that they might be from me, but then you were convinced they were from someone else. Someone I can't even stand."

"He is an idiot, isn't he?" she grinned.

Tom nodded. "Total."

"And I've been a bigger one. It was awful, Tom, I couldn't think of a thing to say and he was so . . . it was so awkward." She sighed and felt Tom's arms go tighter around her. "Every time he moved in closer I found myself saying something to stop him kissing me. And I kept thinking about you with Charlotte." She flushed bright red. "Oh my god! I can't believe I said that."

'Why?" Tom asked, gently stroking her hair. "What do you think I'm going to do?"

She blushed an even deeper shade, her heart pounding so hard she was sure he could feel it through her dress. "I . . . I don't know. . ."

"It's always been you, Alex."

"It's funny . . . I always assumed you'd be there and then I had to think again, imagining you with someone else. I just couldn't let my stupid side let the dumb Chris thing go – and I thought I'd lost you. Now it seems so right, I wonder what I was thinking. Look at us all. It's been the best prom ever.'

"Alex."

"Yes?"

"You're going to stop talking now and I am going to kiss you. OK?"

Alex pressed her lips together and closed her eyes. "OK."

Nothing happened.

"Swear you won't start talking again?"

She kept her eyes shut.

"Swear."

"I mean really, really swear."

"Really, really swear."

"Because I don't want you to start jabbering on just as I move in. You know, like you do."

He put his finger on her lips to stifle her giggle and she felt the room disappear around her until it was just Tom and her, and she could feel his lips on hers and it wasn't like her fantasies – it was so, so much better.

And it really was the best prom ever.

ACKNOWLEDGEMENTS

To my wonderful family and friends for all their support, patience and encouragement, particularly Frances Toynbee and Anna and Lucy Kell who shared so much invaluable information about their own experience of Proms with me.

To my agent Stephanie Thwaites at Curtis Brown and to Helen Thomas and Lena McCauley at Scholastic who made all the enjoyment of writing this book possible.

KEEP READING FOR
PROMTASTIC QUIZZES,
TIPS AND ACTIVITIES!

PROM-PLANNING CHECKLIST

Check all these off before the big day and you'll be totally ready when it comes to prom night.

- ☐ Transport
- ☐ Dress
- ☐ Shoes
- ☐ Bag
- ☐ Accessories
- ☐ Date (optional)
- ☐ Hair
- ☐ Nails
- ☐ Makeup
- ☐ Ticket

EMERGENCY SUPPLIES

Don't forget these! Make room for an emergency pack in your purse, you never know what you might need.

- [ ] Dental floss
- [ ] Mints
- [ ] Plasters
- [ ] Kirby grips
- [ ] Blotting pads
- [ ] Lip gloss
- [ ] Tampons

FIVE IMPORTANT GETTING-READY TIPS

1. Eat a hearty breakfast before you start getting ready. Once you're working on your make-up or rushing to the salon to get your hair done, you might not have time to stop to eat, but there's nothing more important than being well energized so you can dance all night!

2. If you're getting professional help, your nail appointment should be made for the day before prom day and your hair and make-up appointments should be made for the morning of prom. Do a test run and don't be afraid to say if you don't like something.

3. If you're getting dressed at home, plan to get ready with friends – it's way more fun and they can help with the eyeliner that you can never quite get right. YouTube is great for tutorials, but don't pick something so complex that you end up too stressed to enjoy it.

4. Make sure you can put on your dress without smudging your make-up – if you can't step into your dress, consider putting it on before doing your make-up. If you do put on your dress first, you can protect it from stains by wearing a robe or towel on top.

5. Wait to put on your heels until the very last minute. No matter how comfortable they seem at first, even the best heels start to sting by the end of the night. Delay the painful must-take-off-these-shoes moment as long as possible by waiting until just before photos to put on your heels.

NAIL TIPS

Doing your nails on your own? Follow our tips for salon-perfect nails.

Stage One: Preparation

Wash your hands. Then clip and file your nails into your preferred shape (round, square or somewhere inbetween). Soften your cuticles with oil or lotion and push them back (gently!) with a cuticle stick. Exfoliate your hands, wrists and forearms with a hand scrub and then wash your hands one more time to create a clean surface for the nail polish. Make sure to clean under your nails. Use nail-varnish remover or acetone to remove any last impurities from your nail surface before you start any painting. Set up everything you need for the painting stage in easy reach, and make sure you're working on a stable, even surface.

Stage Two: Painting

You might think a base coat isn't needed, but your nails will be better protected and your varnish will stay on longer and look smoother if you use one. It will also hydrate your nails. Wait a full two minutes after applying the base coat, and then apply the first coat of colour varnish. Start by placing a drop of varnish at the centre of the nail, just above the cuticle. Push it down towards the cuticle with your brush and then move it up in a straight line to the top of the nail. Go back to the base of the nail and this time swipe the nail varnish along the right-hand side of the nail, then the left. Make sure to get the brush all the way down to the cuticle and along both sides of the nails. Don't worry if it looks thin, you'll be applying multiple coats. After two minutes, apply the second coat of polish. If the colour is still not as vibrant as you'd like, you can apply a third coat. Lastly, apply a top coat. This is another step you don't want to skip as it prevents your polish from chipping and adds shine. If you're using sparkles, glitter or any other nail accessories, add them before the top coat. The top coat will seal them in and prevent them from being knocked off.

Stage Three: Waiting

Clean up any mistakes by dipping a small brush or toothpick in nail varnish remover and running it along the edges of your nails. Leave your nails to dry for ten minutes, then carefully test them to see if they're dry. This is the hardest part, but there's nothing worse than ruining perfectly done nails by trying to use your hands too soon! Dipping your hands in ice water after they've air-dried for a few minutes can help them dry faster, but make sure to set up the bowl of ice water before you start painting your nails. Watch a movie or TV show while you wait. Once you're sure your nails are dry, enjoy your perfect at-home manicure!

HAIR GUIDE

You've got your dress – but now you have to choose the perfect hairstyle to match! Read the guide below to help you choose a hair style to complement the neckline of your dress on prom night.

Strapless?

There are so many different varieties of strapless gown – sweetheart, V-neck, scoop neck, straight across – and because it's such a versatile style, you can do a lot with your hair as well. You can show off the neckline of your dress with an up-do, or wear your hair loose without worrying about it clashing with straps. With a strapless dress, you have lots of choices, so choose something that fits your personal style!

One shouldered?

If you're wearing a one-shouldered dress, try wearing your hair swept to the opposite side as the strap. A side part, with your hair styled in loose waves or a fishtail plait, will balance out the dress – and it will provide visual interest for all those group photos that will be taken with your side facing the camera.

Thin straps?

Give the straps on your dress a noticeable weight by pulling your hair back. A messy up-do with a few pieces of hair pulled loose at the front will frame your face beautifully, and complement the delicate nature of your dress's straps.

Thick straps?

To balance out the thick straps on your dress, try your hair half-up and half-down. Pinning the hair near the front of your face back will allow the straps to be seen, but leaving the rest of your hair loose will prevent the straps from overwhelming you.

Sleeves?

If your dress has sleeves, they were probably one of the draws of the dress for you, so you won't want to cover them up. This is a great opportunity for an understated up-do – to let the sleeves shine. A low chignon of loose curls or a sleek bun would look beautiful and classic with this neckline.

Something else?

If your dress neckline isn't covered here then it must be unique – do something fun and unusual with your hair to match! Try a high curled ponytail if your dress has complicated straps, wear your hair loose with a few delicate plaits woven in if your dress falls off the shoulder, or go for a giant bun if your dress has a high boat neckline or ties around your neck. Whatever you choose, make sure it's fun and reflects your personality, just like your dress does!

Short hair?

People think there's not a lot to do with short hair, but they couldn't be more wrong. With short hair you don't have to worry about the neckline as much, instead style your hair to compliment your dress in general. Wearing something understated and simple? Straighten your hair and have it neatly styled. Is your dress more elaborate? Then curl your hair or go for a more casual tousled style to complement the complexity of the dress. With short hair you can also have lots of fun with accessories like fresh flowers or clips – they'll be noticeable and striking!

PROM DOs

1. Do give and accept compliments. You look great!

2. Do allow your mum and dad that final cheesy photo. This is a big night for them too.

3. Do hang out with your friends, even if you have the perfect date. Friends are for ever.

4. Do dance the final dance. Even if your feet are killing you, you won't regret it in the morning.

5. Do stand up straight. Everyone looks confident with good posture.

6. Do take pictures. You'll want their help to remember this night for ever.

7. Do leave enough time to get ready. There's nothing worse than being rushed.

8. Do eat something before you leave. Pictures take

ages and you don't want to get hungry.

9. Do thank the organizers. They've been preparing for this night for months and they're worried you won't have fun.

10. Do Relax. Have fun whatever happens. The things that go wrong might be the best stories in years to come.

PROM DON'TS

1. Don't take your heels off until after photos – but don't feel you have to wear them all night either.

2. Don't eat anything with tomato sauce while wearing your dress. Trust us.

3. Don't make any big plans for the next day. You'll be exhausted and need a lie-in.

4. Don't be mean to anyone who asks you to dance. They've probably been plucking up the courage for months.

5. Don't be afraid to ask your crush to dance. This could be your moment.

6. Don't be mean about anyone's dress. Seriously, it's just not cool.

7. Don't get a manicure less than three hours before prom. It WILL smudge.

8. Don't worry if you don't have a date. Going with friends can be just as much (if not more!) fun.

9. Don't worry if you don't look like a celebrity – not even they look perfect in real life.

10. Don't let anyone ruin your fun. This is your night. Enjoy it, however you want to.

PROM AFTER-PARTY IDEAS

Just because prom is over doesn't mean the night is! Any of these fun ideas could be the perfect end to your night and create lasting memories.

Bonfire on the Beach

There's nothing more romantic than sitting around a bonfire, roasting marshmellows. Bring blankets and snacks and sit around chatting with all your friends and listening to the waves.

Movie Night

After standing around in heels and a dress all evening, nothing is better than lounging in pyjamas, rehashing all the gossip and snacking on popcorn. Invite all your girlfriends and stay up until sunrise.

Brunch Party

There's something extra delicious about breakfast foods at midnight. And after all that dancing you're bound to be hungry! Plan a waffle party with loads of toppings and let everyone make their own.

PROMTASTIC QUIZ

Which Promtastic girl are you? Take the quiz below to find out if you're an Alex, Leigh, Charlotte, Grace or Kristyn.

1. **Prom night is approaching, how do you feel about it?**
   a) You've been waiting years for this! You're on the prom committee and you can't wait to help make it a perfect night for everyone
   b) Ugh, you're really not sure whether you want to go or not
   c) You're looking forward to it, but you're worried about looking right and finding a date
   d) Dresses, boys, friends, fun! You're excited, but you have butterflies in your stomach too
   e) You think it'll be fun, but it's not the most important thing in your life right now

2. **What would your dream date involve?**
   a) An amazing three-course romantic dinner and seeing a show

b) There are so many options – maybe a gig or an adventure of some sort – as long as it's not boring or clichéd

c) You'd love your date to choose what you do – a surprise would be romantic

d) Definitely a picnic, followed by rowing on a lake, ending with dinner in that cute new restaurant in town

e) Something low-key – what you talk about is more important than where you are

3. Which role do you play in your friendship group?

a) You're the organiser, the one who makes things happen

b) You're the quiet leader, even if you don't always want to be

c) You're the listener, always there for everyone

d) You're the disorganised-but-loving one

e) You're whoever your friends need you to be

4. What are you most likely to be doing on a Friday evening?

a) An extra-curricular activity or volunteering

b) It depends, but probably not at the party that half your year group is at

c) At a house party with a big group of friends, but sometimes you'd secretly love to be in your pyjamas drinking hot chocolate, if only you weren't worried about missing out

d) Having a sleepover with your closest friends, watching movies and eating popcorn

e) At dinner or seeing a movie with either your bf or bff

5. What do you want to do when you finish school?

a) Something in the city – you want excitement and a bustling diary. Perhaps PR for a huge fashion label or working at an advertising agency

b) Whatever you end up doing, it'll be because you're doing what you want to do, not what everyone expects you to

c) A lawyer, doctor or other high-flying professional – you hope you have what it takes...

d) Maybe something creative, or with animals or children – as long as you can give back to the world in some way

e) Your parents want you to be a doctor, but you're not sure. There are so many things you want to explore. You worry you might not choose the right thing

6. How do you react to stressful situations?

a) Tell yourself not to get emotional! You need a plan. You make a list and start checking things off
b) Ignore the problem – it'll go away
c) You work well under pressure – you have it under control
d) You hate stress and get a little overwhelmed sometimes
e) You put on a brave face even though you might feel the opposite inside

7. Which form of transport would you choose to turn up to your prom in?

a) A helicopter would be great – something special and spectacular
b) Well if you do go, you'll choose something unique like a motorbike or quad bike
c) You don't really mind – you'll do what everyone else is doing

d) A vintage car – you love the thought of all those happy couples travelling in it over the years

e) A chauffeur-driven limo with all your friends

8. What's inside your bag right now (other than the usual keys, money, phone...)?

a) Everything you could possibly need! But one thing you always have is the lucky trinket that you've had for years

b) Snacks, mascara and a copy of The Bell Jar

c) Notepad, lipstick, phone and a bar of chocolate – that combo will solve any problem

d) A diary, a leaking pen and loads of mementoes (receipts, ticket stubs, photos...)

e) Your grandmother's locket – you love having it, but it's not really you

9. Which word appeals to you the most?

a) Success

b) Originality

c) Hope

d) Romance

e) Truth

10. The boy you had a crush on has asked your friend to prom and she said "Yes". How do you feel?

a) You're hurt but keep it to yourself – you'll put your energy into finding a new date

b) You feel betrayed by your friend, but convince yourself it's a good thing – this boy was clearly not right for you

c) You're angry – it feels like a rejection from both your friend and the boy

d) You're devastated – you've spent months imagining how prom would be if you were together

e) You're a little sad but you hide it – if your friend is happy that's the most important thing

11. What's your greatest fear?

a) Failing your exams

b) Being no different to everyone else

c) Being left out

d) Being alone

e) Not being able to live the life you really want

Mostly As – you're like Leigh!

You're the top of the class and you're passionate about everything you do – which is a lot, and it pays off! Your friends rely on you to make sure there's always a fun plan in the diary, and if there are any problems, you're usually the one to fix them. You get a little annoyed sometimes that others don't seem to pull their weight as much as you do, but really, if you're honest with yourself, you wouldn't have it any other way. Sometimes you get a bit too caught up in trying to make everything and everyone perfect, including yourself. In fact, you're harder on yourself than anyone, which is something lots of people don't realize about you because of your composed exterior. But you're a perfectionist because you see the potential in everything. You want everything to shine in the way you know it can! Try being a little easier on yourself from time to time and take a moment to pause and enjoy the brilliant friendships and achievements you've created.

Mostly Bs – you're like Charlotte!

You're creative, self-aware and you love being an individual – you refuse to conform to something just because everyone else does. People really admire the way you're not afraid to be yourself, even if you're not always what's considered "cool". You love variety and adventure and you're always looking for the latest band or trend that no one else has heard about yet. Sometimes you get so caught up in trying to be different that you can be a little hard on those that go along with the norm. You often feel like people don't understand you, which is hard, because you really understand yourself, much better than most people. It can make life lonely at times, but if you open up a bit to others and let yourself enjoy the wide range of experiences life has to offer, you might find that people understand you more than you imagine. And when you truly open up to people, you are capable of deep and lasting friendships and relationships.

Mostly Cs – you're like Kristyn!

You're spontaneous and fun (even playful) and you love to be at the centre of all the action. In fact, it's hard for you when you're not, and sometimes you can get a bit anxious about being left out. Because you understand what that feels like, you're the person who really stands up for the underdog. People see you as strong, loyal and compassionate – qualities that you have in abundance, especially when you stop worrying about what people think and just let your true self shine through. It can take you a while to choose what beliefs to commit yourself to because there's always so much to consider, but once you have, you follow through with conviction. It can therefore sometimes be hard for you to admit you're wrong, but if you realize you've made a mistake you'll do everything you can do make it right. You've been hurt in the past, and it can be difficult to let yourself trust people, but have some faith in yourself and others – you're the best friend or girlfriend anyone could have.

Mostly Ds – you're like Alex!

You're caring, optimistic and a true romantic. Your main priority in life is finding love. That doesn't always mean romantic love, because you also have great friendships and you're really close to your family – in fact, you couldn't cope without them. You constantly worry about others, and this makes you a natural confidant, and you're the person they turn to when they need a shoulder to cry on. This sometimes means that you neglect your own feelings, though, because you always put others before yourself. Deep down, it's hard to admit, but you can feel a little resentful that others don't always see when you need help in return. Even though you're surrounded by people, you can feel alone. But when you find that special person, when romance enters your life, it will be everything you dreamed of, because you'll make it so. Hold out for the person who truly deserves all the love and attention you have to offer.

Mostly Es – you're like Grace!

You're easy-going, stylish and charismatic, and that means you're popular. School, friends, success ... it all comes easily to you. People are drawn to you like bees to honey, which is lucky, because you love being surrounded by people – you hate being alone. You love the deep connections that you're able to make with others, but sometimes you feel that those around you expect you to be perfect, and that can be tiring – you just want to live your life truthfully, being able to relax without being in the spotlight. You know who you are, but you're not always brave enough to let it show. However much you want to let go of the image you've so carefully built up, it's also hard to take risks and really be true to who you are. You're afraid that if people really knew you, they would disappear from your life. But have courage – the real you is the best you and people are desperate to see her.

You got a bit of everything?

That's OK! That's because you're just you! You're still figuring out who you are and who you want to be, and you have plenty of time to find out what really matters to you. Also, everyone changes from day to day. You might be a Grace one day and a Leigh the next. It's hard sometimes not to quite understand yourself, especially when those around you seem to be so sure. But they're probably not. They're probably as unsure as you are. Take a breath, stop worrying about what you're not and enjoy the journey to finding out what really makes you tick. Experiment with things that excite you or inspire any curiosity – or even scare you. The scariest moments can be the greatest learning experiences too. Don't worry about not fitting into a box – you're you, and that's all that matters.